Thomas Blacklock

Remarks on the Nature and Extent of Liberty

as compatible with the genius of civil societies - on the principles of

government and the proper limits of its powers in free states

Thomas Blacklock

Remarks on the Nature and Extent of Liberty
*as compatible with the genius of civil societies - on the principles of government
and the proper limits of its powers in free states*

ISBN/EAN: 9783337382049

Printed in Europe, USA, Canada, Australia, Japan

Cover: Foto ©Andreas Hilbeck / pixelio.de

More available books at **www.hansebooks.com**

ON THE

Nature and Extent of LIBERTY, as compatible with the Genius of CIVIL SOCIETIES;

On the Principles of GOVERNMENT and the proper Limits of its Powers in Free States;

And, on the JUSTICE and POLICY of the AMERICAN WAR.

OCCASIONED BY

Perufing the OBSERVATIONS of Dr PRICE on thefe Subjects.

In a LETTER to a FRIEND.

Benefacere reipublicae pulchrum eft.; etiam benedicere haud abfurdum.

EDINBURGH:

Printed for W. CREECH; and T. CADELL, London.

M,DCC,LXXVI,

My Dearest Friend,

YOUR laft letter, which I received in due time, contains fuch a number of inquiries, both literary and political, that, defpairing of abilities or leifure to anfwer the whole, my prefent obfervations muft be confined to one topic. According to your defire, I have obtained, and with the ftricteft attention perufed, *The Obfervations on the nature of Civil Liberty, on the Principles of Government, and on the Juftice and Policy of the War with America, by Richard Price,* D. D. F. R. S. and fhall give you my opinion of them, with as much candour as the nature of the fubject, and the fenfibility of my temper, will admit.

As the principles upon which my fentiments are founded, will likewife be delineated, you may judge for yourfelf, whether the conclufions drawn from them are fairly deducible or not. It muft give every generous mind pain to think, that the author has had fo much reafon to complain of abufe. In the courfe of thefe animadverfions, perfonal reflection fhall be avoided with all imaginable care, if the fpirit and intention of the performance does not deferve and extort them : But, as the objects of our difquifition are national, it is not propofed, nor can it be incumbent on any writer, to obferve the fame delicacy in fuppreffing national ftrictures. The emotions which public conduct, when reviewed, will naturally infpire ; the jealoufy of civil liberty, which has kindled our author's zeal to a height, perhaps, more confpicuous than laudible and expedient, may apologize for the freedom with which my opinions and fentiments are delivered. They were originally intended for your own private ufe ; but you are at liberty, either to communicate or fupprefs them, as you fhall think proper. Their publication, indeed, may, perhaps, irritate the voice of cenfure againft me. Parties are ever jealous of their confequence, and ready to diffeminate fufpicions, which may invalidate or difappoint the efforts of fuch as oppofe them. But thefe cafual impreffions neither infpire me with terror nor concern. If ever my name and perfon fhould be difcovered, it will be obvious to the world, that every motive which impels the mercenary or ambitious to write, muft have operated a quite contrary effect upon my mind; and that the only principles which could either engage or animate my prefent attempts, are juftice and benevolence.

Lucrative

Lucrative or honorary premiums may have charms for such authors as are conscious of relish, and capacity to enjoy them. For my own part, were I more contiguous to the channels in which those advantages flow, I should survey them with that indifference, which every man must naturally feel, whose duty and inclination concur to fix his views rather on a death of honour, than a life of pleasure. But these preliminaries have already detained us too long from the contemplation of our author.

> Together let us beat this ample field,
> Try what the open, what the covert yield ;
> The latent tracts, the giddy heights explore
> Of all who blindly creep, or sightless soar :
> Eye Nature's walks, shoot Folly as it flies,
> And catch the manners living as they rise.
>
> Pope.

I must add, that the task would be endless perpetually to quote the Doctor in his own words. His arguments may often be more concisely stated, with equal force and perspicuity. But, for your own satisfaction, it will be necessary to retain his pamphlet constantly in your eye; that if, in these recapitulations, his meaning should either be injured or perverted, whether from inadvertency or prejudice, you may be able to confront and detect such misrepresentations, by comparing them with the original itself.

The Doctor, in his preliminary observations, informs us, that our American colonies, persuaded, at last, of the intention of Great Britain to deprive them of that liberty, which is the natural and unalienable right of all states and communities, are determined rather to run every hazard, and suffer every calamity, than to lose it. He considers it, therefore, as a question of great importance, to examine whether such a persuasion be reasonable or not. This profound and solemn scrutiny he undertakes with sensible reluctance ; as, in performing the severe, but salutary operation, he must be urged by strong feelings to deliver sentiments incompatible with the measures of that government under which he lives, and of which, according to his own declaration, he has always been a constant and zealous partizan. Charity will prompt you to believe, that the Doctor may consistently revere the persons, whilst he disapproves the measures of his governors. Such patriotic paroxysms, as the strong feelings which he mentions, though rarely observed in life, are certainly possible in nature, and might, therefore, necessitate a private and unconnected man to show his detestation of the public procedure in the most conspicuous light, and strongest colours which he could use. But the spirit and tendency of his observations are the only premisses from whence you can, with certainty, conclude that loyalty to government, that detach-

ment

ment from party, which he fo fanguinely profeffes. Perhaps you may
think it ftrange,'that a conftant and zealous well-wifher of government
fhould, at a crifis fo important as he thinks the prefent to be, throw
obftacles in its way, which can have no other effect than to retard
its motions, and diffufe incendiary maxims, which can have no
other tendency but to inflame the rage, or multiply the number of
its enemies. It may poffibly furprife you no lefs, that a man fo
private and unconnected, fo abfolutely free from the fpirit and principles of a faction, fhould, in all his political views and fentiments,
coincide with the minority ; but this muft be attributed to the invincible force of truth, which is too univerfal to be concealed, and
too confpicuous to be miftaken. This will appear more evident
from a nearer profpect of the Doctor's plan. Once for all, however, let me repeat my injunction, that his treatife may be conftantly before you when reading this letter ; becaufe, otherwife,
it will be impoffible for you to judge whether his meaning is fairly
reprefented or not; and, confequently, what degree of validity the
objections here offered againft him can be allowed to poffefs.

He tells us, that, before the queftion between us and the Americans can be clearly and ultimately decided, we muft form correct ideas of liberty. It is indeed a mafterly ftroke in the political
conduct of our patriots, both at home and abroad, to bring liberty
into the queftion. When the venerable genius, the facred pa-
tronefs of our conftitution, is threatened with infult or violation,
what wonder if every living foul fhould be fired to madnefs, in a
cauie fo glorious and interefting ! But, from the Doctor's own principles, we hope to fhow, however ftrange it may feem, that liberty
has not the leaft concern in the matter.

SECT. I. Since, however, the difcuffion of Britifh and American affairs, in the Doctor's opinion, fo effentially depends upon
proper notions of liberty, it naturally becomes his firft concern, to
explain what he means by this public, this ineftimable blef-
fing.

> Non fumum ex fulgore, fed ex fumo dare lucem
> Cogitat, ut fpeciofa dehinc miracula promat,
> Antiphatem, Scyllamque, et cum Cyclope Charybdin.
> HOR.

> He does not lavifh at a blaze his fire,
> Sudden to glare, and in a fmoke expire ;
> But from a cloud of fmoke he breaks to light,
> And pours his fpecious miracles to fight ;
> Antiphates his hideous feaft devours,
> Charybdis barks, and Polyphemus roars.
> FRANCIS.

To

To illuſtrate his notion of liberty, the Doctor is not contented with one general definition, adapted to every ſituation in which a voluntary agent may be placed; but conſiders the attribute of freedom as applicable to each of theſe ſituations in particular. This leads him to contemplate liberty as either phyſical, moral, religious, or political, according to the various views in which a ſpontaneous and ſocial agent may be regarded.

' By phyſical liberty, he means that principle of ſpontaneity, or
' ſelf-determination which conſtitutes us agents ; or which gives us
' a command over our actions, rendering them properly ours, and
' not effects of the operation of any foreign cauſe. Moral liberty,
' he underſtands to be the power of following, in all circumſtances,
' our ſenſe of right and wrong; or of acting in conformity to our
' reflecting and moral principles, without being controuled by any
' contrary principles. Religious liberty, he defines to be the power
' of exerciſing, without moleſtation, that mode of religion which
' we think beſt ; or of making the deciſions of our own conſciences,
' reſpecting religious truth, the rule of our conduct, and not any
' of the deciſions of others. In like manner, according to him,
'. civil liberty is the power of a civil ſociety or ſtate to govern it-
' ſelf by its own diſcretion, or by laws of its own making, without
' being ſubject to any foreign diſcretion, or to the impoſitions
' of any extraneous will or power.'

Upon this ſubject, the reverend politician ardently wiſhes, if poſſible, to fix our thoughts, not only as of infinite moment in itſelf, but as the ſource from whence thoſe principles are to be drawn, by which he means to convict Great Britain of exorbitant claims, and tyrannical procedure, with reſpect to her American colonies. But, ſurely, if he had been ſufficiently attentive to the lubricity of that ſtation, from whence he intended to open the campaign, he would have diſcovered more caution, in deducing all the ſubſequent modes of liberty from an origin ſo metaphyſical as that which he has ſelected. He ought to have been aware of the inſuperable difficulties, which muſt occur to every profound inquirer, in his attempts to aſcertain the phyſical freedom of man. Does he not know, that metaphyſical writers have affirmed no mechanical powers in nature to be more neceſſary in their operations than the conduct of man? Has he not read, that ſenſations of pleaſure and pain are continually obtruded on the mind from external objects, which ſhe neither can repel nor change? Has he not been told, that motives reſult from ſenſations, by laws no leſs immutable than the neceſſity by which ſenſations reſult from objects? Has it not been reiterated by all the ancient and modern neceſſitarians, that the powers of choice and volition are no leſs infallibly determined by a prepollent motive, than any mechanical balance by a preponderating weight ; inſomuch, that a being ſufficiently acquainted with the ſeries of cauſes and effects, may, with abſolute certainty, determine

termine the conduct of any given human character, in any given circumstances ? But of thefe fubterfuges we fcorn to take advantage. Religious, moral, and civil liberty, are not words without meaning, but excite clear and definite ideas in the intellect, and correfpondent feelings in the heart of man We therefore meet the Doctor upon his own ground, and with his own weapons. But, as he acquaints us, that what has been formerly premifed was particularly intended for the illuftration of civil liberty, to that auguft and important object let us with him direct our views. Civil liberty, then, in his own words ' is the power of a civil fociety or ' ftate to govern itfelf by its own difcretion, or by laws of its own ' making, without being fubject to any foreign difcretion, or to ' the impofitions of any extraneous will or power.'

Every civil fociety is compofed of individuals ; each of thefe individuals has diftinct powers of volition and difcretion within itfelf. The volition, therefore, of any civil fociety, muft be the aggregate or final refult of all the volitions and difcretions in its component parts. If, therefore, every particular conftituent of the fociety be as free as poffible, the whole fociety muft be free ; and, vice verfa, if the whole community be under any oppreffion or conftraint, all the individuals of which it is compofed muft be proportionably oppreffed and conftrained. But, if emergencies fhould occur, either from the internal oeconomy of any ftate, or from its connections and negotiations with other ftates, in which, for want of powers to judge of the matters in queftion, many of the individuals can neither exercife volition nor difcretion, but muft of neceffity fubmit to the difcretion, and act by the volitions of others, I would gladly afk the Doctor, Whether, according to his analogical reafoning, or fubfequent definition of civil liberty, thefe individuals can be politically free, in any cafe where it is poffible for political and perfonal freedom to take different directions? The Doctor feems fenfible of fome inextricable difficulties in the fyftem of political liberty which he propofes ; and, therefore, after having infifted, that civil liberty is effentially included in the internal power of a ftate to govern itfelf, he prudently refolves that felf into a majority. But who, in the name of all thofe inherent and indefeafible perfonal rights, with which of late our preffes have groaned, and our roftrums have thundered, who invefted this arrogant majority with a legitimate power, not only to fuperfede the volition and difcretion of the minority, but to obtrude its own volition and difcretion upon them? In fuch a conjuncture, there muft be a manifeft violation of perfonal or phyfical liberty For the people, whofe opinions and inclinations are thus fuperfeded, muft not only remain in tame and paffive acquiefcence, but frequently act in full oppofition to their own fentiments and principles. Still, therefore, I demand, from whence a majority could derive fuch unbbunded pre-eminence ? It could not even be conferred by the confent of thofe who were to be governed. For liberty, in its moft comprehenfive meaning, is the indelible character of our being, the natural and unalienable right of man. But if this right be unalienable, no voluntary refignation can, in any degree, deprive us of its poffeffion. Hence, every individual member of a ftate muft perpetually remain invefted with all thofe powers, which could be claimed or exerted by him, before he was incorporated in that community. He is as effectually empowered to act for himfelf in a legiflative, executive, or facerdotal capacity, as if thofe privileges had never been refigned to the ftate of which he is a conftituent. But what if it fhould happen, that the number of individuals, whofe difcretions and volitions can have no public operation, for want of powers to judge of the matters in queftion, or even to act by their native light, upon judgments previoufly formed, in reality conftitute the majority of a ftate? What if the hand of nature, in the diftribution of her gifts, has authorifed and eftablifhed this difparity of powers and faculties? What if the exigencies of every ftate demand a fubordination of offices, and, confequently, an inequality of the talents, whether natural or acquired, which are neceffary for difcharging them? What if the menial tafks, the laborious and fevere manoeuvre of life, fhould indifpenfibly require this multiplicity of hands? And what if the Wife Providence of that Beneficent Being, who created and difpofed the various parts of the univerfe, fhould have intended this difference of qualifications and employments uniformly and univerfally to fubfift? What, then, muft be done? We muft contract our fupreme and all-comprehending majority to a number immenfely fmaller than that of which it was originally compofed. For this our author, heaven blefs him, has provided a remedy. He is fenfible how difficult it muft prove to collect the fuffrages of a national majority, when the affair in agitation is of fuch a nature as to threaten abfolute abortion, unlefs propofed with fecrecy, refolved with expedition, and executed with vigour. Such emergencies in the government of ftates are by no means unfrequent; and whoever reads the hiftory of mankind with attention, will obferve numberlefs inftances, in which enterprizes rafhly undertaken, unfteadily purfued, or tardily executed, have produced the moft fenfible difadvantages, and fometimes the utter ruin of the ftate by which they were adopted. From all this it will plainly appear, that our Utopia cannot confift of a numerical majority. For all the individuals who are confcious of inability, either to determine or to act for the ftate, without the impulfe and direction of fuperior talents, muft transfer their powers to a majority, comprehended or included within the majority fpecified by Dr Price; and as diverfities in the human frame, whether arifing from conftitution or education, or both, muft neceffarily occafion differences of opinion, this minor-majority muft acquiefce in the fentiments of a majority

ftill

ftill inferior to itfelf. Thus we find, that the powers of deliberation and execution in a ftate muft either be miferably exerted, or confined to a number much lefs than the majority originally affigned by our author. But how is this inferior majority authorifed to perform the offices of government? There appears no method by which it can affume this privilege, unlefs by violence, by hereditary authority, or by popular election. For, in this promifcuous ftate of human affairs, the inherent advantages which one man may poffefs above another, are not fufficient to acquire him that influence which his qualifications may deferve, or the exigencies of the ftate require. But fuperior might has no legitimate claim to govern; for, if it had, the ideas of law and liberty would at once be annihilated, and the dictates of brutal force become the only rules of implicit obedience. Neither can fuch a power be hereditary; for it is by no means a perfonal property, and, therefore, cannot be mechanically transferred from generation to generation. If *falus populi fuprema lex* be efteemed an axiom in politics, (which the gentleman whom I now oppofe will not probably difpute), it muft inevitably follow, that no perfon can be invefted with power and authority, who is not pre-fuppofed able and willing to ufe them for the public good. But, as we have been taught by bitter and repeated experience, that wifdom and virtue do not flow in the current of blood, nor are conveyed in the fame manner with names and eftates, it is evident, that no hereditary claim to legiflative authority can merit the fmalleft degree of public regard, if the reprefentative be not properly capacitated and qualified to difcharge that office, for which he is a candidate. It has indeed been pretended, that men contract habits of obedience to one particular family, which can neither be eafily nor quickly reverfed. But the common occurrences of life will immediately difcover the fallacy of this principle, and fhow, that the human mind can neither be inured to obedience, nor continued in it, except by the real or fuppofed merit of their rulers. Hence it appears, that, where no objection can be urged againft the heir of a family, his defcent, his education, and the example of his anceftors, will influence the people to receive him. But, if he fhould be found effentially difqualified, either by vice or imbecillity, for the ftation to which he afpires, he is rejected without fcruple. Precedents of this conduct in public life are fo frequent, and fo obvious, that it would be fuperfluous to quote them. The only alternative, therefore, left us, by which men can be invefted with public authority, is the fanction of public choice. This, we acknowledge, has never been formally difputed by our author. But ftill we fhould be curious to know, How it is reconcileable with the natural and unalienable right of perfonal freedom? He who, in any cafe, authorifes a fubftitute to judge or act for him, by that deputation virtually refigns the power, or, if you pleafe, the freedom of acting or judging for himfelf. Thus it appears, that perfonal freedom, in particular emergencies, may be refigned. How far this refignation may be carried, the exigences of the ftate alone can determine. For if, by confcious inability to judge and act for themfelves, the members of any ftate are induced to chufe a reprefentative, who may be better qualified to difcharge thefe offices, How can the perfons by whom they were elected, either determine how far that power muft be extended, or at what period it ought to be refumed ? Thefe, and other public meafures of a fimilar nature, muft be projected and ratified by a majority of reprefentatives alone, and can be no longer fuppofed in the power of their conftituents. For, if thofe by whom they were originally chofen were eftablifhed in a proper fituation, and endowed with proper qualities to limit the exercife and duration of delegated power, it is plain, that they could not have the fmalleft reafon, either from the nature of things, or accidental circumftances, to delegate their power; or, in other words, to chufe reprefentatives at all. It is plain, that the internal oeconomy, or external tranfactions of any ftate, muft proceed upon general principles. But the laws which general views and principles can only infpire and fuggeft, muft, for the fame reafon, be general. In every general inftitution, the particular interefts, exigences, and fituations of individuals, muft frequently be overlooked, and fometimes fuperfeded, in favour of the diffufive advantage which is the object of the general law. Since, therefore, the fubjects of deliberation in a ftate are general, the reprefentatives chofen for particular diftricts, or by certain bodies of men, ought not to terminate their views and interpofitions in the advantage of thofe bodies by which they are conftituted alone; the common-wealth, in its full extent, is their primary object; and the particular accommodation or advantage of thofe leffer communities, by which they are conftituted, only a fecondary confideration. Hence it is evident, that, though particular reprefentatives fhould never loofe fight of the intereft of their conftituents, but rather reconcile and adjuft them with the general welfare and profperity; yet, in reality, they fhould be more properly confidered as the guardians and reprefentatives of the whole ftate, than of any fingle proportion of land, or quantity of men contained in it.

From what has been faid, it will appear to be neither expedient nor practicable, that conftituents fhould, at pleafure, retract the powers with which their delegates are invefted; but there is no medium between retracting the power, and obeying its injunctions. Every government, where there is no dernier refort, muft of neceffity either, diffolve and return to primaeval anarchy, or be like motion in a circle, which, by continually returning upon itfelf with equal preffure, remains in abfolute fufpenfe. Now, fince there is no cafe within the limits of wifdom and juftice, to which legiflative authority cannot extend, and no alternative but obedience left

to

to fubjects, on all fuch occafions, it is clear, that, in every govern-ment, there muft be a political omnipotence. No perfonal right can be more facred than that of felf-poffeffion. For this reafon, the Habeas Corpus act is one of the nobleft and moft inviolable barriers of Britifh liberty. Yet, on more occafions than one, that act has been fufpended; and it has been permitted to apprehend the per-fons of men not only without the due forms of law, but without affigning any caufe of fufpicion. Such a ftretch of power, in the ordinary courfe of affairs, would have been efteemed equally capri-cious and tyrannical. But, when the fafety of a threatened con-ftitution demanded the temporary abrogation of this law, however facred, however productive of general fecurity, the fufpenfe of its operation was wife, meritorious, unavoidable. In political, as in commercial navigation, there are undoubtedly rocks, quickfands, and fhallows, towards which if the veffel be fteared, the mariners have a right, if they can, to ftop her courfe, and call her pilots to account. If any legiflature fhould enact fuch laws as are fubverfive of that very conftitution from whence it derives its power, it is guilty of political fuicide, and its members are feverely accountable to public juftice. But dangers, which require fuch violent and ge-neral interpofition, muft be vifible to heaven and earth : They muft not be exhibited to the public eye by the fpirit of faction, the ma-lignity of fuperftition, or the fafcination of intereft. Their reality and extent muft be univerfally felt, otherwife refiftance is a viola-tion, a daring and execrable violation, of the moft facred ties and effential interefts by which fociety can either be conciliated or u-nited.

It has of late been a favourite topic amongft our pretended patrons of liberty, that rebellion and loyalty are denominated, not by their nature, but by their fuccefs. They affert, that the pro-moters of the glorious and happy revolution, by which the crown was transferred from the lineal heirs of the houfe of Stewart to the Prince of Orange, had been branded, under the former reign, with the opprobrious title of Rebels, and would ftill have been regarded as fuch, if their attempts had proved abortive. It is by no means eafy to decide, whether fuch maxims excite a higher degree of con-tempt, by their palpable and ridiculous abfurdity, or of horror, by their malignant and diabolical tendency. It cannot be denied, that unhappy confequences, through all the annals of human nature, have flowed from civil government ; but thefe are by no means its neceffary and genuine effects. On the contrary, it is conftituted, by God and nature, the parent of fafety, the nurfe of virtue, the guardian of property, and of every thing dear or facred amongft men. Curfed, therefore, beyond the poffibility of human execra-tion, curfed is that infamous wretch, who, from malice, wanton-nefs, or lucre, attempts to oppofe or retard its legitimate exercife. It muft already appear to every unprejudiced eye, that, though power and right are not, as Mr Hobbs would make them, the fame
thing;

thing ; yet the latter always prefuppofes the former, nor can pof-fibly fubfift without it. It is true, that a perfon unjuftly imprifoned may have a right to be free, becaufe he has a natural capacity of freedom, and is guiltlefs of every mifdemeanor which might render it neceffary for fociety to confine him. It is likewife true, that, prior to every compact or declared choice, all men, who are properly qualified, have a right to judge and act for themfelves But it cannot be admitted, that a lunatic parent has a right, either to the adminiftration of his fortune or family. When the powers of dif-charging thefe functions ceafe, the natural right of exercifing them muft be abfolutely extinguifhed, though law has found it expedient to fuppofe the exiftence and validity of fuch rights uniformly con-tinued. No man, therefore, can claim by right the exercife of any talent, whether natural or acquired, of which he is not actually poffeffed. Power or capacity are the natural and indifpenfible bafis of every right ; nor can the one exift without the other. For I beg to know, What is a right, more than the authorifed exertion of power, or poffeffion of property? The diverfity of authorities from which rights are derived, may occafion fome difpute concerning their nature, their validity, their extent, or their permanency ; but every claim of right neceffarily prefuppofes and implies a power or capacity in the perfon who affumes any prerogative to inforce or enjoy it. Nor is this all ; for every native right can only belong to its poffeffor, in proportion as he is qualified to exercife or enjoy it. In all external inftitutions, it is frequently impracticable, and ftill more frequently inexpedient, to inveftigate or afcertain the degrees of power or capacity upon which rights are eftablifhed; for this reafon, the external rights of individuals, and even of communi-ties, muft retain their full validity, without regarding the peculiar circumftances by which the powers of exerting, or capacities of enjoying them, may be circumfcribed. But, where fuch fcrutinies are poffible and neceffary, even the external right will be limited, according to the degrees of power or capacity found in him who is invefted with it. If, then, the powers of determination and ac-tion, fubfifting in individuals, be found unequal to the tafk of judging and acting for the whole, and, for that reafon, be tranf-ferred to delegates, whofe qualifications are prefumed adequate and proper for fuch a truft ; on the fame account, thefe powers muft remain in the fame hands where they were originally depofited, till the general voice of the legiflature fhall prefcribe their duration and extent. For, as the fafety and advantage of particulars are necef-farily included in the fecurity and profperity of the whole, the plan purfued by government muft be confiftent, uniform, and per-manent. But this end it is impoffible to accomplifh, whilft indi-viduals imagine themfelves at liberty to exercife or refume their rights at pleafure.

We

We have already found, that the delegates chofen by particular diftricts or commuuities, are firft to be regarded as concerned for the whole ftate, and anxious to promote its moft extenfive interefts; fo that the local reprefentation to which they have been elected is only a fecondary province. It cannot therefore be imagined, that the moft inconfiderable member of a free ftate is without reprefentation in its legiflature. For, though a number of individuals may neither be entitled by their internal qualifications, nor their external importance, to have any immediate influence in the choice of a reprefentative, yet the office to which they are elected, extending not only to the whole diftrict, but to the whole ftate, muft intereft fuch members of the legiflature for the welfare of every individual, as far as it is compatible with the good and profperity of the whole. Hence it is evident, that, in a free government, every perfon is either actually or virtually reprefented. But, granting that, on particular or critical emergencies, the decifions of a legiflature, thus conftituted, may be wrong, and even oppreffive, How are thefe errors to be corrected? How are thefe misfortunes to be redreffed? Not by appeals to the great majority of the whole ftate; for fuch attempts would be equally impracticable and ineffectual. Not by impofing temporary or occafional reftraints upon the legiflative or executive powers: For, allowing that any authority fubfifted in a ftate fufficient to impofe thefe reftraints, ftill the remedy would be worfe than the difeafe.

Thus we have found, Firft, That the natural rights of men, even to perfonal liberty, are not abfolutely inherent or unalienable; otherwife there could be no government. Secondly, That, if individual rights are alienable, fuch conceffions may be made to the ftate of which we are members, as are either neceffary to its fubfiftence, or productive of its real and permanent utility. Thirdly, That the majority, by which the ultimate decifions and final refults of government are projected and ratified, cannot be the great majority in which thefe powers are invefted by Dr Price; but muft be confined to a majority of delegates ftill much inferior in number to that by which they are chofen. Fourthly, That the rights of fuch delegates are neither to be refumed nor limited, in an arbitrary manner, by the conftituents, but muft of neceffity be extenfive and permanent, to produce the order and welfare of the political fyftem. Fifthly, That, in every legitimate government, there muft be an *incontrollable* or irrefiftible power; becaufe, without fuch a power, the government muft either be fufpended or diffolved. The difference, therefore, between defpotic and free governments, is not, that fuch a power fubfifts in the former, but not in the latter; for every government, in its ultimate determinations, muft be effentially abfolute, and can fubfift no longer than its injunctions are implicitly obeyed. But it feems, if fuch a power muft be exerted by every government, our author can make no diftinction, whether it fhould be lodged in one or many hands, except that the tyranny is more infupportable when exerted by bodies of men, than by one individual. The Doctor, however, forgets, that divided power can never act with the fame force as when collected in one hand. He forgets, that the ends of a fingle tyrant may be more eafily accomplifhed than thofe of many; becaufe a particular defpot will only purfue one end at a time ; whereas, amongft many, the meafures of ftate muft perpetually be diftracted, by the multiplicity of views and interefts purfued by each individual, and that, till thefe can be rendered compatible, the motions of government towards any given point can never be uniform and regular; and, confequently, no tyranny can operate with the fame malignity as when invefted in one perfon. Befides, when the affairs of government are tranfacted by delegates, thefe reprefentatives are connected in their moft effential interefts with thofe by whom they are conftituted, and fubjected to the fame laws which they themfelves enact for others. Strange! that a defender of America fhould forget this view of government ; but it was for the intereft of his caufe rather to omit it here, that it might be afterwards refumed with greater advantage. If the conclufions now deduced fhould appear extraordinary, or even harfh to thofe who now are fo clamorous, and would gladly feem fo diftractedly enamoured of liberty, it is hoped they will meet with a more favourable reception from every modeft inquirer, when he hears what may be farther faid concerning the nature of a ftate, or a civil fociety. This is a theme upon which our author has not beftowed one fingle reflection. Yet he has not drawn any particular inference, in favour of the Americans, from his principles of phyfical, moral, religious, or civil liberty, which can be pronounced conclufive in the fmalleft degree, till the idea of a civil fociety be afcertained, and its nature underftood. For if, according to the principles which conftitute a civil fociety, or what the ancients called *Patria*, it fhall be found, that America and Great Britain are not different civil focieties, but conftitute one and the fame ftate, it will be allowed, That no ufurpation of fupremacy is obtruded upon them by aliens and ftrangers : That the Britifh empire internally retains the power of governing itfelf ' by its own difcretion, or by laws of its own ma-' king; without being fubject to any foreign difcretion, or to the ' impofitions of any extraneous will or power :' That the Americans, if not actually, are virtually reprefented in the parliament of Great Britain : That no taxes are extorted from the Americans without their own confent, by meafures more violent or unjuftifiable than thofe to which their fellow-fubjects in Great Britain willingly and properly fubmit : That America has no more title to refift the injunctions of the fupreme legiflature than any county or borough in Great Britain ; and that the war proclaimed againft the colonies by their mother-country is juft, expedient, and political.

Amongft

Amongſt political writers, it ſeems to be too frequently taken for granted, that the idea of a country is generally and thoroughly underſtood: Yet nothing is more certain, than that few, extremely few, give themſelves the trouble to aſcertain what they mean by a country, or from whence ariſe the prepoſſeſſions which, in virtuous boſoms, are ſo naturally, ſo warmly excited by that tender and ſacred name. Aſk the generality of mankind what they mean by a country, and you will find, that, though the attachment which they feel is immenſely diſproportioned to the cauſe which they diſcover, yet their ſpeculative notions of a country extend no farther than the ſoil, the climate, and other ſenſible phaenomena of the ſame kind; yet theſe external and mechanical prepoſſeſſions, by a feeling heart, and a cultivated underſtanding, are eſteemed the weakeſt ties which bind us to our country. For, as the Roman philoſopher tells us:

Cari ſunt parentes, cari liberi, propinqui, familiares : Sed omneis omnium caritates patria una complexa eſt : Pro qua quis bonus dubitet mortem oppetere, ſi ei ſit profuturus ?

‘ How dear to our ſouls are our parents, how dear our children,
‘ our relations, our intimate acquaintance? yet all the tender ſen
‘ timents with which nature inſpires us for each of theſe, are com
‘ prehended and felt at once in the love of our country. Where,
‘ then, is the man of virtue who would ſcruple to ſacrifice his life
‘ for the advantage of an object ſo tender and important, if its in
‘ tereſt could be promoted by his fall?’ *Cic. de officiis.*

Theſe ſublime ſentiments are by no means the unintelligible rant, the romantic whims of a philoſophical viſionary. They are recognized by every uncorrupted heart in every age. Can any one, therefore, imagine that a country is merely local, and comprehends no more than the ſenſible objects contained within a certain limited ſpace? The geographer and annaliſt may indeed delineate countries by the rivers, lakes, and mountains which diverſify the ſurface of the globe; but the moral agent conſiders his country as the ſphere of action within which his moſt important exertions are circumſcribed, and his nobleſt affections concentred. The biaſes impreſſed on his mind by nature and habit, in favour of particular places, though, in ſome degree, they may be felt and approved, are languid and impotent, when compared with that more exalted ardour, thoſe ſublimer and nobler emotions inſpired by the ſociety in which he has been formed and educated. Local prepoſſeſſions, indeed, are far from being uſeleſs; they are the original hints of nature to awaken our tenderneſs, that, by proper gradations, our affections may be expanded, and conducted to objects more adequate to their capacity, and more worthy of their dignity. But theſe ligatures are neither ſufficient to hold the parts of a political ſyſtem together, nor to produce thoſe ineffable agitations of ſoul which ariſe from the different viciſſitudes of a country. You aſk me, then, What is a

country ? or how diftinguifhed from thofe fortuitous and temporary affemblages of men, which the Englifh denominate *Herds*,
and the French *Peuplade*. ? For there muft undoubtedly be fome
principles of union, by which the one is diverfified from the other.
It is plain, therefore, that there are fuch things as national characters. I do not at prefent enter into the difpute, Whether this general
fimilarity of temper and genius arifes from natural and mechanical,
or from internal and moral caufes. If you wifh to carry this re-
fearch farther, you may confult L'Efprit des Loix, liv. 14. chap. 2.
and Mr David Hume'. Effay on National Characters.

To explore the fources of thefe local diverfities, could have no
effect in elucidating the prefent difputes. It fuffices, for my purpofe, that the fact is univerfally admitted. We have therefore in-
veftigated one principle of union, by which civil focieties are preferved from capricious or arbitrary diffolution. Befides, all the
members of any ftate, each according to his different province, are
urged by neceffity, and influenced by education, to regard public
and private fecurity as productive one of the other, and to purfue
one common intereft, fometimes even at the expence of their own
perfonal advantage; becaufe the facrifices they make refult in the general good, of which they, as individuals, conftituent of the general
fyftem, may afterwards participate. By their foil, their climate,
their infular or continental fituation, they are directed what natural productions may be cultivated, or what exotics introduced with
fuccefs. Hence their employments, whether of fifhing, hunting,
paftoral occupations, agriculture, or manufactures, are in a great
meafure common. By the character and genius of the neighbour-
ing ftates, by their own internal demands, and by their native ac-
tivity or indolence, their difpofition for peace or war, their different kinds of commerce, and their various negociations, are confiderably affected. Hence, their inclinations, their efforts, their
habits, are univerfally diffufed. Few of the pleafures or entertainments of life are folitary. Relaxation is abfolutely neceffary for
the prefervation of nature; nothing is more contagious than the
tafte for amufement—Hence their feafons of repofe, and the different kinds of recreations which they purfue, are in a great meafure
uniform. When their intercourfe, their laws, and their fentiments, are confirmed by time and habit, while their duration has
been fufficient to produce noble actions, or ftriking viciffitudes recorded in hiftory or commemorated by public monuments, the
conduct of their anceftors, the prepoffeffions and ufages tranfmitted
by precept and example, have the moft aftonifhing effect, in producing and confolidating their union. To all thefe, if we add the
ties of blood and nature, the attachments of friendfhip, vicinity,
and acquaintance, the reciprocal obligations arifing from an inter-
change of focial offices, the ideas of pleafure or advantage affociated
with places of common refort, we fhall find, that nature and providence

vidence have amply provided for the union, and, confequently, for the fubfiftence of ftates. But the moft efficacious principle, by which the fubfiftence and integrity of a country can be preferved, is the common belief of one religion, wife in its inftitutions, and benevolent in its fpirit.

Thus I have enumerated the moft powerful and effential caufes which form and preferve a country. Other accidental circum-ftances may co-operate with no fmall degree of efficacy. As na-ture, however, through all her works, delights in uniformity a-midft variety, and in tempering them fo nicely that one may not deftroy the other; fo we find the fame univerfal law no lefs confpi-cuous in her moral, than in her mechanical productions. Hence it is, that the national character, and almoft every other principle of union in ftates, admit of confiderable diverfities, which, in general, are far from being fubverfive of the fyftems where they o-perate, and, in particular cafes, may produce the moft falutary and beneficent effects. Thus, befides the ftaple commodities of the na-tion, particular diftricts may produce peculiar articles of traffic, which enlarge the fphere, and diverfify the employments of com-merce. Thus, even the collifions of religious fectaries, when the principles of divifion are not effential, and the ftruggles moderate, may affift in preferving the general warmth and fincerity of devo-tion. Thus we may fee, that minute diverfities of characters, opi-nions, and interefts, when limited with difcretion, and managed with propriety, are never deftructive of a ftate, but may frequent-ly prove falubrious, and beneficial in their confequences.

That you may not imagine thefe ideas of national union peculiar to myfelf, I fhall quote you the fentiments of a philofopher, highly refpectable for his morals, in which my own will be found either expreffed or implied.

' Of all human affections, the nobleft and moft becoming hu-
' man nature, is that of love to one's country. This, perhaps,
' will eafily be allowed by all men who have really a country, and
' are of the number of thofe who may be called a People, as en-
' joying the happinefs of a real conftitution and polity, by which
' they are free and independent. There are very few fuch country-
' men or freemen fo degenerate, as directly to difcountenance or
' condemn this paffion of love to their community and national
' brotherhood. The indirect manner of oppofing this principle is
' the moft ufual. We hear it commonly as a complaint, that there
' is little of this love extant in the world. From whence it is haftily
' concluded, that there is little or nothing of friendly or focial affec-
' tion inherent in our nature, or proper to our fpecies. 'Tis how-
' ever apparent, that there is fcarce a creature of humankind who
' is not poffeffed, at leaft, with fome inferior degree or meaner fort
' of this natural affection to a country.

C

' 'Tis a wretched afpect of humanity which we figure to our-
' felves, when we would endeavour to refolve the very effence and
' foundation of this generous paffion into a relation to mere clay
' and duft, exclufively of any thing fenfible, intelligent, or moral.
' 'Tis, I muft own, on certain relations, or refpective proportions,
' that all natural affection does in fome meafure depend. And, in
' this view, it cannot, I confefs, be denied, that we have each of
' us a certain relation to the mere earth itfelf, the very mould or
' furface of that planet, in which, with other animals of various
' forts, we (poor reptiles) were alfo bred and nourifhed. But, had
' it happened to one of us Britifhmen to have been born at fea,
' Could we not therefore properly be called Britifhmen ? Could we
' be allowed countrymen of no fort, as having no diftinct relation to
' any certain foil or region ; no original neighbourhood but with the
' watery inhabitants and fea-monfters ? Surely, if we were of law-
' ful parents, lawfully employed, and under the protection of law ;
' wherever they might be then detained, to whatever colonies fent,
' or whitherfoever driven by any accident, or in expeditions or ad-
' ventures in the public fervice, or that of mankind, we fhould ftill
' find we had a home, and country, ready to lay claim to us. We
' fhould be obliged ftill to confider ourfelves as fellow-citizens, and
' might be allowed to love our country or nation as honeftly and
' heartily as the moft inland inhabitant or native of the foil. Our
' political and focial capacity would undoubtedly come in view,
' and be acknowledged full as natural and effential in our fpecies,
' as the parental and filial kind, which gives rife to what we pecu-
' liarly call Natural Affection. Or, fuppofing that both our birth
' and parents had been unknown, and that, in this refpect, we
' were in a manner younger brothers in fociety to the reft of man-
' kind ; yet, from our nature and education, we fhould furely e-
' fpoufe fome country or other, and, joyfully embracing the pro-
' tection of magiftracy, fhould of neceffity, and by force of nature,
' join ourfelves to the general fociety of mankind, and thofe, in par-
' ticular, with whom we have entered into a nearer communication
' of benefits, and clofer fympathy of affections. It may, therefore,
' be efteemed no better than a mean fubterfuge of narrow minds,
' to affign this natural paffion for fociety and a country to fuch a
' relation as that of a mere *fungus*, or common excrefcence, to its
' parent-mould, or nurfing dunghill.' *Shaftesb. Charact. vol.* 3.

Thus, having treated, with as much minutenefs and precifion,
concerning the general principles of government, and the nature
of civil fociety, as appeared neceffary for my purpofe, before I come
to grapple more clofely with the Doctor, permit me to make a few
general obfervations with refpect to Great Britain and America.
And, *firft*, I would gladly know, what nation beneath the canopy of
heaven retains more confpicuous features of its defcent, more obvious and durable marks of its origin, than America ? Have they
not

not preferved the manners and cuftoms of Britain, even to its provincial dialects? Should an American crofs the Atlantic, and land any where upon the continent of Europe, Would he not, unlefs he chofe to correct the miftake, be univerfally taken for an Englifhman? And, on the contrary, fhould an Englifhman travel into thofe parts, where the Americans are better known than the Britains, Would he be diftinguifhed from an American? Inconfiderable differences there may be, in their complexions and manners, but lefs obfervable than thofe by which people of the fame country, in different diftricts, are decerned one from another. Do not moft of the Americans, who boaft an oftenfible origin, (for fome have more than ordinary reafons to avoid the ftudy of heraldry), acknowledge, with pleafure and exultation, their defcent from Great Britain? Are not their internal police, and their laws in general, as conformable to thofe of Great Britain as their fituation and circumftances will admit? Were not the powers given to their affemblies and councils intended merely to redrefs fuch inconveniences, and to anfwer fuch exigences, as the parliament of Great Britain, by reafon of its diftance, could not fupply? Was not the power of negation, depofited in the hands of their native legiflature, an obvious and indelible acknowledgment of its fupremacy? Have not other pofitive acts of the fame legiflature been received in America, with that general acquiefcence which, in every political fyftem, is, and muft be, interpreted as a legal and plenary confent? Are not their commercial interefts intimately, I had almoft faid infeparably, united with thofe of Great Britain? Is there any other ftate in Europe in which they can repofe the fame degree of confidence, and with which they can form the fame coalefcence in trade? Is there any other European nation with which they can be fo unanimous in their political principles, even when the differences which now fubfift between Britain and America are admitted in their full extent? Are not their progenitors, their friends, their acquaintances, ftill in Great Britain? Are not the general principles of religious eftablifhment the fame in both, though the clerical fubordination and epifcopal hierarchy, by law eftablifhed in England, have not yet been extended to America? In a word, if the pamphlets which continually iffue from their preffes, if the addreffes and petitions of their congreffes, whether provincial or continental, may be regarded as the authenticated fenfe of the people, Do they not loudly and repeatedly acknowledge themfelves our fellow-fubjects, our brethren, our countrymen? We grant that fuch acknowledgments are no more than the occafional and temporary dictates of fear or intereft. But, whatever figns of intention may be admitted in private contracts or domeftic coalitions, language will ever be the fole interpreter, as it is the only poffible medium of political negotiations. By language, therefore, the parties engaging will ever be reckoned ftrictly and implicitly bound, if treaties impreffed with
the

the public fanction imply any obligation at all. Political relations are more permanent, and lefs fluctuating, than thofe of nature itfelf. The Americans, therefore, cannot be our brethren, our fellow-fubjects, our countrymen, only when their purfes or perfons are in danger. Thefe relations are either abfolutely chimerical, or muft continue to fubfift when their circumftances are profperous and fecure. Will any man pretend to affirm, that, when the union was formed between Scotland and England, the fame fimilarity of genius and character, the fame coincidence of views and interefts, the fame conformity of taftes and fentiments, the fame analogy of cuftoms and inftitutions, the fame unanimity in religious principles, could be invefligated between thefe two hoftile nations? Yet our pacific and benevolent anceftors imagined that fuch a coalefcence might be attended with important and reciprocal advantages. They flattered themfelves, that ungrateful names, and invidious diftinctions, might be effaced or obliterated, by the endearments and accommodations of mutual intercourfe. They were tranfported with the pleafant anticipation, that, in procefs of time, the people, like their ifland, might become one, and every native, inftead of recognizing any particular diftrict, might claim the whole of Britain as his country. Nor was this plan chimerical or impracticable : For, though the diverfities which characterized the Scots and Englifh were, at that time, more confpicuous, and lefs reconcileable, than thofe which now diftinguifh America from Britain, yet, as thofe differences were rather the effects of contingency than of nature, it was prefumeable that they might at laft be forgotten. Scotland, though funk from the glory, the dignity, the influence of an independent kingdom, to the impotence and obfcurity of a defpicable province, might at laft have acquiefced in her abject deftiny, and tamely fubmitted to oppreffion, when inflicted without the intolerable aggravation of infult. But how could humanity, politenefs, or decency, be expected from a' nation inebriated with glory and fuccefs, which it neither had qualifications to deferve, nor wifdom to enjoy with moderation? How could it be expected that they would exert virtues and decorums towards others, which were unknown amongft themfelves? Their names, indeed, have been adapted and naturalized from foreign languages, and Englifh lexicographers have endeavoured to explain them. But, as it was impoffible for thefe authors to infpire the fentiments which the words were intended to fignify, they could only teach their countrymen to affociate one articulate found with another. When a treaty of union had been folemnly ratified by the fupreme councils of both nations, it was natural to belieeve, that the motives from which their mutual conceffions proceeded, fhould have influenced the minds of the people to confirm, by internal amity, the conjunction which civil utility had begun. If the Scots had it in their power, in a ftate of feparation, either to be troublefome enemies, or ufeful neighbours;

neighbours ; upon thefe principles, they became objects of confideration to the Englifh. Had that country poffeffed the magnanimity, the generous enlargement of foul, which, without ever exhibiting it conftantly, arrogates the weakneffes and infirmities of a lifter kingdom, inftead of provoking infult, fhould have claimed humanity and protection. Which of thefe conducts the Englifh have purfued, let heaven and earth be judges. In the mean time, it muft be confeffed, that the leaft important of thofe circumftances, by which they were originally difunited, was infinitely more efficacious in continuing and increafing political divifion, than mere local diftance, which is the only characteriftic upon which our opponents fix, as the permanent and capital diftinction between Great Britain and America. Had we indeed been feparated from them by vaft tracts of land, and by numerous interpofing nations, the diftance might then have been an object formidable to us, and the proximity of America to other ftates might have induced them to form alliances with fuch people as were more acceffible than we. But, whilft we are only intercepted by a fafe and navigable ocean, the diftance, to every political purpofe, is in a great meafure annihilated ; and its inconveniences may be entirely removed, by the internal expedient of councils and affemblies, without being productive of national feceffion. If thefe pofitions are, as they muft be, allowed by our antagonifts, will they not reflect, with fhame and confufion of face, upon the impudence and fophiftry of their declamations, when they infift, that mere contiguity, or diftance of place, can have any effential influence, either in conftituting or dividing a country ? But we come now more particularly to examine the force of the Doctor's arguments.

SECT. II. Thus far we have attended to the Doctor's definition of liberty alone, and found it incompatible with the nature of government. It is therefore with good reafon that we have recourfe to the ideas of an author, more enlightened in the theory of human nature, and, confequently, better acquainted with the principles of government than his Reverence, though he fubjoins D. D. F. R. S. to his name. The perfon I mean is, the Baron de Montefquieu, from whofe excellent differtation on the Spirit of Laws, liv. xi. chap. iii. and iv. I muft beg leave to prefent you with the following profound and rational account of liberty in his own words.

' CHAP. III. *Ce que c'eft que la Liberté.*

' IL eft vrai que dans les democraties le peuple paroît faire ce
' qu'il veut : Mais la liberté politique ne confifte point à faire ce
' que l'on veut. Dans un etat, c'eft-a-dire, dans un fociété ou il y
' des loix, la liberté ne peut confifter qu'à pouvoir faire ce que
' l'on

‘ l'on doit vouloir, et à n'etre point contraint de faire ce que l'on
‘ ne doit pas vouloir.

‘ Il faut fe mettre dans l'efprit ce que c'eſt que l'indépendance,
‘ et ce que c'eſt que la liberté. La liberté eſt le droit de faire tout
‘ ce que les loix permittent ; et ſi un citoyen pouvoit faire ce
‘ qu'elles defendent, il n'auroit plus de liberté, parce que les autres
‘ auroient tout de même ce pouvoir.

‘ Chap. IV. *Continuation du meme Sujet.*

‘ La démocratie et l'ariſtocratie ne font point des etats libres par
‘ leur nature. La liberté politique ne fe trouve que dans les gou-
‘ vernmens moderés ; mais elle n'eſt pas toujours dans les etats
‘ moderes. Elle n'y eſt que lorfqu'on n'abuſe pas du pouvoir :
‘ Mais c'eſt une experience eternelle que tout homme qui a du pou-
‘ voir eſt porté à en abuſer ; il va juſqu'à ce qu'il trouve · des li-
‘ mites. Qui le diroit ! la vertu même a befoin de limites.

‘ Pour qu'on ne puiſſe abuſer du pouvoir, il faut que par la dif-
‘ poſition des chofes le pouvòir arrête le pouvoir. Une conſtitution
‘ peut être telle que perfonne ne fera contraint de faire les chofes
‘ auxquelles la loix ne l'oblige pas, et à ne point faire elles que la
‘ loi lui permet.'

Thus tranſlated. ‘ It is true, that, in a democracy, the people
‘ feem to act agreeably to their will : But political liberty does not
‘ confiſt in being able to do what we will. In a ſtate, that is to fay,
‘ in a fociety where there are laws, liberty can only confiſt in be-
‘ ing able to do what one's will ought to determine, and in not be-
‘ ing conſtrained to do what one's will ought not to determine.

‘ It is neceſſary to impreſs on our minds what is independence,
‘ and what liberty. Liberty is the right of doing every thing which
‘ the law permits : And if a citizen had it in his power to do what
‘ it forbids, he would poſſeſs liberty no more ; becauſe all the reſt
‘ of his fellow-citizens would be equally intitled to the fame pri-
‘ vilege.

‘ Democratic and ariſtocratic governments are not free by their
‘ own nature. Political liberty is not to be found but in govern-
‘ ments where thefe are judicioufly blended and tempered : But it
‘ fubſiſts not always even in ſtates which are ruled with moderation.
‘ In fuch it is no longer recognized than whilſt men abſtain from
‘ the abufe of power : But it is a dictate of eternal experience, that
‘ every man poſſeſſed of power has a propenſity to abufe it ; he pro-
‘ ceeds ſtill farther and farther, till he perceives the limits of his
‘ career. Who would imagine it! virtue itſelf is under a neceſſity
‘ of being limited.

‘ That

' That no perfon may be able to abufe his power, it is neceffary
' that, by the arrangement of the conftitution, one power fhould
' be a check upon another. A conftitution may be fuch, that no
' perfon fhall be conftrained to do any thing to which the law does
' not oblige him ; and, at the fame time, he may be hindered from
' doing thofe things which the law permits.'

It feems, then, that the definitions of liberty formerly received,
are not fo exceptionable as Dr Price may think them. Nay, it appears to me indifputable, that, though all the particular, occafional,
and temporary volitions of all the individuals which compofe a ftate
could be collected and digefted, yet, till they are promulgated by
public authority, till they are armed with proper fanctions, and impreffed with genuine fignatures of authenticity, they have neither
right nor force to command obedience. But when the volitions of any majority, properly conftituted, are publifhed, and confirmed by legiflative authority, from that period they become laws.
Independent of focial obligations, every man is at liberty to regulate his perfonal affairs, by the determination of his own will, in
the laft refort. Thefe volitions are laws to him; but can be fuch to
no one elfe. Multiply coincident volitions to any number you
pleafe, they may become motives to induce our compliance, but
never ftatutes to compel our obedience, till publifhed and authorifed by that legiflature to which we belong. A free government,
therefore, (whatever our author, or others, intoxicated with fan-
cyful ideas of liberty beyond the power of hellebore, may perfuade
themfelves), is a government of laws, not of men. Thefe laws
may be fufpended or reverfed by the fame power which gave them
exiftence and fanction ; but this power can never be in the majority of any people, whilft that fubordination of talents and employments, originally conftituted by nature, fubfifts. A pure democracy, therefore, where all are equally invefted with fupreme authority, and all equally fubjected to controul, being an oeconomy
fubverfive of itfelf, and incompatible with the circumftances of human nature, is abfurd and impoffible. It is not number or fituation alone which creates the difficulty of collecting and balancing
the fuffrages of a people ; it is the abfolute incapacity of the many,
in every ftate, to give their voices upon queftions in which their
fpirits have neither been illuminated by nature, nor can be in-
ftructed by art. I do not affirm that nature and fortune have always acted in concert, even in a point fo tender and important as
this. We have learned by frequent and mournful experience, that
the moft eminent talents, the moft extenfive powers, precluded from
the means of culture in their progrefs, and of operation in their
maturity, have been deftined to languifh in the deep and perpetual
obfcurity of private life.

Perhaps

Perhaps in this neglected spot is laid
  Some heart once pregnant with celestial fire ;
Hands, that the rod of empire might have sway'd,
  Or wak'd to extasy the living lyre.

But Knowledge to their eyes her ample page,
  Rich with the spoils of Time, did ne'er unroll ;
Chill Penury reprefs'd their noble rage,
  And froze the genial current of the soul.

Full many a gem of purest ray serene,
  The dark unfathom'd caves of Ocean bear ;
Full many a flow'r is born to blush unseen,
  And waste its sweetness on the desart air.

Gray's Elegy in a Country Church-yard.

But, though we lament catastrophies of this kind, when they are discovered, we cannot admit that their number bears any proportion to a majority, nor allow such facts, however deplorable, to have any influence in estimating the powers of the multitude in any state. It remains, therefore, an indubitable maxim, that the uncultivated vulgar, whose original powers, and mechanical employments, render them as little susceptible of political ideas and speculations, as of mathematics, or any other abstract science, can have no power, and, from what has been formerly said, can have no inherent right, either to will or judge for the state, but by delegation ; and some of them only possess that right in consequence of the inexpediency which is ever found in detecting their want of qualities, by which alone it can be claimed.

Power, then, though constituted for the public good, though no more than the powers of the many collectively exerted, and properly directed to public order and happiness, as its ultimate end, can never be the creature of the people in general: For no being, or aggregate of beings, can possibly bestow or transfer what they do not possess. If, then, personal liberty be to act according to the determinations of a man's own will, and political freedom a conduct, not inspired by these determinations as they really are, but as they ought to be ; it follows, that personal and civil liberty may take different directions, and that licentiousness, being a violation offered by personal freedom to civil liberty, is therefore liberty in excess. But would Dr Price, in reality, persuade us, that power is the creature of the people? I thought Christianity had instructed us better. I thought it taught us to derive the origin of legislative authority from God alone, as its genuine and primaeval source, and that power is no less a trust deposited by God in the hands of the people for their own happiness, than by the people in the hands of their delegates. This truth, indeed, will appear demonstrably evident to every one,
who

who admits the exiſtence and ſuperintendency of an infinitely good, wife, and powerful Being; for ſuch an adminiſtration muſt either remain inflexibly neuter, in all the viciſſitudes of human affairs, or be peculiarly concerned in the conduct of ſtates and empires. If this is true, the people are more ſtrictly accountable to God for their choice, allowing them to be capable of chuſing from rational motives, than their delegates can poſſibly be to them for the moſt flagrant acts of mal adminiſtration. From hence it is evident, that whoever rebels againſt the legitimate ordinations of civil government, rebels againſt God himſelf: Nor would the ſame execrable impiety forbear to violate the order of eternal and univerſal monarchy, if not reſtrained by the impoſſibility of ſucceſs, and the horror of puniſhment. Evident as theſe principles may be, from the nature of God, and the conſtitution of man, they derive additional force and luſtre from the Chriſtian diſpenſation. To one who believes the authenticity of revealed religion, the queſtion is irreverſibly decided by the annunciations of eternal and immutable veracity. For tho' the ſcriptures do not inform us, that the perſons and minds of men can be abſolutely appropriated by any individual of the ſpecies, tho' they by no means authoriſe the tyrant in acts of cruelty and deſpotiſm; though they never taught, that kingdoms, like goods and chattles, were transferrable, by hereditary right, from generation to generation; yet they ſolemnly and indiſpenſibly enjoin us, to obey the lawful mandates of powers lawfully conſtituted. They aſſure us, not only that government in general, but that particular forms and offices of government, are ordained by God.

' Let every ſoul be ſubject unto the higher powers. For there is
' no power but of God: The powers that be are ordained of God.
' —Whoſoever, therefore, reſiſteth the power, reſiſteth the ordinance
' of God: And they that reſiſt ſhall receive to themſelves damna-
' tion.—For rulers are not a terror to good works, but to the evil.
' Wilt thou then be afraid of the power? Do that which is good,
' and thou ſhalt have praiſe of the ſame. For he is the miniſter of
' God to thee for good. But if thou do that which is evil, be a-
' fraid; for he beareth not the ſword in vain: For he is the mini-
' ſter of God, a revenger to execute wrath upon him that doth evil.
' Wherefore ye muſt needs be ſubject, not only for wrath, but alſo
' for conſcience ſake.—For, for this cauſe pay ye tribute alſo; for they
' are God's miniſters, attending continually upon this very thing.
' —Render, therefore, to all their dues: Tribute to whom tribute
' is due, cuſtom to whom cuſtom, fear to whom fear, honour to
' whom honour.' *Rom.* 13. *verſes* 1. 2. 3. 4. 5. 6. 7.

If, then, there be no power but of God; if the powers that be are ordained of him, How is power the creature of the people? How does it originate with them? And how are they entruſted with its ſupreme direction? It is owned, that God may make the people his inſtruments in the diſtribution of power; but it is nei-

D   ther

ther originally created, nor ultimately directed by their choice, no more than the channels through which a fountain flows can be called its fource. They are indeed vehicles of paffage, and lines of direction, but have no influence in producing the waters which they convey, and are no more than merely inftrumental in facilitating the bias which the ftream purfues.

It will not be eafy to judge, whether an ingenuous mind feels greater fhame or forrow, when under the neceffity of confronting a Chriftian and a clergyman with a portion of fcripture fo clearly fubverfive of his political axiom. If he knew no better, Why did he betray his ignorance ? If he was apprized of this paffage, and its meaning, Why does he not renounce his character and function ? He tells us, that the diftinction between licentioufnefs and defpotifm, is no more than this, that, in one cafe, the perfons and properties of men are in danger from an arbitrary tyrant, and, in the other, from a lawlefs mob. One fhould have imagined, that the Doctor might have treated the people with more profound refpect than to call them a *Mob*. Rouffeau fhould have taught him better manners. That eloquent, but fingular author, feems to infinuate, that it is impious to inflict the appellation of a mob upon any collection of human beings, without reflecting of what materials it is compofed.

If the gentlemen who talk fo highly of a majority, and fo contemptibly of a mob, would be confiftent with themfelves, they ought certainly to follow Rouffeau's advice. To me there appears no difference, previous to every political convention, whether tacit or expreffed, between what, at one time, they call a *People*, and at another, a *Lawlefs Mob*. In effect, that very multiform idol, which, in one form or arrangement, they devoutly adore, is the *bellua multorum capitum*, which, in another, they feem to hate or defpife. Yet here it is, according to Dr Price, that political omnipotence muft be lodged, if there be fuch an uncontrollable power in government. Hail then! hail then! thrice hail, Almighty Mob! I imbibe thy fury ; I feel thy impetuofity ; I reverence thy hoarfe and various clamour. But, amidft the diverfity and inconfiftency of thy decrees, Which muft I obey ? Whither fhall my efforts be directed ? What revolution is it thy auguft pleafure to accomplifh ? Muft thy magiftrates and enemies be butchered ? Muft courts of juftice be reduced to afhes ? Muft palaces and temples be plundered and demolifhed ? Thefe are the general occupations of the mob, and this the glorious animation which prevails amongft them. If Dr Price feels fo much charity, if he is fo favourably preoccupied for a fpirit of rapine and carnage, he cannot give a more ftriking teftimony of his partiality to that humour, than by offering his perfon as the willing fubject of its operation.

Nor is it fo manifeft as he feems to imagine, that defpotifm is more dangerous than licentioufnefs. It muft be confeffed, that ar-

bitrary

bitrary government, when artfully managed, long protracted, and armed with terror, produces habits of servility in the people, from which it may be difficult, or perhaps impoſſible, to recover them. But theſe are accidental, not natural evils. They may be prevented in their formation, or checked in their career. All extremes, however, have a direct tendency each to its oppoſite. Deſpotiſm or licentiouſneſs naturally reſolve into anarchy, and the general reſult of anarchy is deſpotiſm. For, in ſuch a ſituation, the individuals deprived of common protection, and ſtimulated to madneſs or deſpair, by the intollerable evils which they mutually ſuffer and inflict, have neither capacity and deliberation to ſelect the beſt form of government, nor to arrange themſelves in that order which ſuch a conſtitution requires. In theſe circumſtances, the readieſt means of redreſs, the ſimpleſt political coalition, appears the moſt eligible ; for its immediate advantages are felt, its remoter conſequences ſcarcely foreſeen. Thus, with blind precipitation, they plunge into the gulf of ſervility and arbitrary power. You cannot fail to ſubſcribe, with all your conſenting ſoul, the panegyric of liberty with which our author concludes his ſecond ſection. But you will likewiſe reflect, that he might have ſaved himſelf the trouble, as the taſk has been often performed with nobler enthuſiaſm, and more diſtinguiſhed abilities, than he has diſcovered.

SECT. III. Our ſage author, after having taught us, that liberty is, in all caſes, inſeparable from actual volition, and placed the dernier reſort of government in thoſe who are incapable to govern, proceeds, with equal wiſdom and impartiality, upon the principles of liberty which he had formerly eſtabliſhed, ' to examine the au-
' thority of one country over another.'
Amongſt ſtates, originally diſunited and independent, which, in the revolutions of human affairs, have been ſubjected one to another, by ſuperior force, or other contingences, his reaſoning will frequently be found concluſive. But, when the characters, intereſts, and circumſtances of men, however locally diſtant, conſpire to form one civil ſociety, or even render it more eligible to all concerned, that they ſhould be thus embodied, rather than totally diſjoined, the Doctor's arguments entirely loſe their force, and, by their miſapplication, become pernicious and ſophiſtical. Yet, as ſome of them may be ſpecious and popular, they may claim a degree of attention, which, by their intrinſic force, as adapted to the ſtate of affairs between Britain and America, they never could deſerve.
It ſeems, then, according to the Doctor, that the only bond of civil union, is a juſt and adequate repreſentation. By a juſt repreſentation, he muſt underſtand ſuch a one as is conſtituted by popular election ; otherwiſe his inſeparable conjunction between liberty and volition muſt be violated. By an adequate repreſentation, he muſt
mean

mean fuch a one as, in its number and qualifications, is proportioned to the importance and extent of the bodies which is reprefents. But, in Great Britain, and perhaps in every free flate, not above one-third of the people are reprefented by delegates of their own election. The immediate conftituents of thefe delegates, according to our author's notions of liberty, are free, becaufe the reprefentative chofen by them is the real or fuppofed organ of their, volitions. But in every inftance, however minute, where the reprefentative deviates from the will of his electors, the phyfical or. perfonal freedom, even of the conftituents themfelves, is deftroyed; and the enjoyment of what he calls political liberty, can no more be a compenfation to individuals for the lofs of perfonal freedom; than favours conferred by one ftate upon another can be thought, an adequate recompence for the lofs of political liberty.

In every particular cafe, therefore, the freedom of individual conftituents is as unalienable by them, as political freedom, in general emergences, by the ftate. No man, then, is bound to receive the refults of deliberation, authenticated by reprefentatives which he himfelf has chofen, as obligatory laws, unlefs they coincide with his own particular volitions; and, confequently, no legiflation by representatives can have any force to extort the obedience, even of its own conftituents, except when it is the vehicle of all the various, occafional, and temporary volitions, which are formed at the fame time by every individual, from whofe choice it derives its authority and fanction. But, if the freedom of thofe who conftitute fuch a reprefentation, be a thing fo fubtile and precarious, what muft we think of theirs who have no voice in electing a reprefentative ; fince neither the men employed in government, nor the meafures purfued by it, have the fanction of their choice, How, upon our author's principles, can they be free? Yet furely he muft admit, that, when the Britifh conftitution was in its purity, thofe who were entitled to give their fuffrages for members of parliament, did not amount to above one-third of the people; the other two, therefore, muft be flaves. For it has been formerly remarked, and muft again be repeated, that local diftance or contiguity is nothing to the queftion.

Unlefs, then, it be found, that the political compact equally fubfifts through all ranks of the ftate, and that, by its means, thofe who are not actually, muft be virtually reprefented, What difference can it make, whether the people inhabit a region divided by fenfible boundaries, or quite uniform ; whether they inhabit a region known by the fame or different names? If the actual and perfonal choice of the people be the only criterion between liberty and fervitude, thofe who are not permitted to interfere in fuch elections muft be flaves, to whatever country they belong, and under whatever conftitution they live. Perhaps our fanguine votaries of boundlefs liberty, may think the fenfe of the people fufficiently expreffed

preffed by the fhouts that tear the concave, and the caps that in-
tercept the light of heaven, during the ferment of electioneering.
But one may venture to pronounce, that a proper quantity of wine,
punch, or ftrong bear, liberally diftributed, will engage this venerable majority to exclaim, with the higheft patriotic enthufiafm,
Beelzebub for ever, huzza! Nor is this the character of any particular
multitude, in any particular period or fituation ; for every mob, at
every time, and in every place, is the fame.

Still the Doctor's obfervations prefuppofe the abfolute dominion
of one ftate over another, not the legitimate rule which a mother-
country exercifes over her colonies. Nothing, indeed, can be more
analogous to the natural relation between a parent and a child, than
the political relation between a country and its colonies. To the latter,
from their infancy to their maturity, through every period of their
progrefs, the tuition, the protection, the beneficence of the former
is neceffary. And as, during the minority of children, parents
have a right to the product of their labours, which, however, de-
creafes, as the offspring rifes to the capacity of independence, and
the powers of felf-government : Thus a parent-ftate has a right to
demand from its colonies all the returns which they can properly
make, for her maternal care and liberality, till the fame crifis of
their political exiftence arrive.

When the Doctor obferves, that the flavery of one ftate fubjected
to another is worfe, on feveral accounts, than any flavery of private
men to one another, or of kingdoms to defpots within themfelves,
he feems to have miftaken the policy of ftates inured to conqueft
and domination. They know better things than to govern their
fubjects, or, if you pleafe, their vaffals, by the fame legiflature
with themfelves. No ; they rule them with delegated fway. They
prudently depofit the power in one hand, that its force may be exerted in one direction, and produce the accomplishment of one end:
Did the Roman people govern their diftant provinces by the fame
fenate, the fame confuls, the fame tribunes, to whom the adminiftration of the city was entrufted ? On the contrary, they fent governors, who were accountable to them for tyrannical exactions, or
other mifdemeanors of which they might be culpable. Thus, ' the
' infamy was not fhared by a number,' but fell with all its weight
upon one devoted head.

It were to be wifhed, for the honour of human nature, that the
fellow-feeelings, fuppofed by our author to fubfift between private
men and their flaves, were more confpicuous and beneficent in its
effects. But, furely, thefe fympathetic ideas were not deduced
from the conduct of American planters towards their negroes.

Thefe humane mafters continually exhibit, to the view of God
and man, fuch fpectacles of pain and horror as are fufficient to diffolve heaven in tears, and fill earth with amazement. Yet, not
contented with exercifing all the powers of inventive cruelty upon
the

the living and paffive fubjects of their malice and caprice, they a-
pologize for fuch acts of atrocity as the devil himfelf might bluſh
to acknowledge, by affirming, that, without fuch difcipline, obedience cannot be extorted. God of Juftice! Father of Mercy! How
long fhall thy flumbering vengeance permit fuch daring crimes to
pafs with impunity! Thefe are the fellow-feelings for their flaves,
which our idolators of liberty beyond the Atlantic at prefent
exert, and have all along exerted. Yet who more clamorous againſt
the fhadow of oppreffion, when prefented in diftant profpect, by
the terrors of a heated imagination, than they?

It is pretended, that laws have been enacted in America, and
tranfmitted to the Britiſh parliament, for preventing this execrable
traffic, which were rejected in favour of a commerce fo lucrative.
But, had thefe philanthropic laws been infpired or dictated by
the fpirit of the people, what power in earth or hell could force
them to purchafe thofe miferable wretches, when imported? The
humanity of England has long been highly praifed and piously be-
lieved, becaufe the immediate view of mournful objects infpires
them with a momentary and mechanical pity. But who, that un-
derftands human nature, can perfuade himfelf that thefe generous
difpofitions, thefe tender expanfions of the foul, are founded upon
principle and habit in a nation, where a trade fo execrable in itfelf,
and fo difhonourable to nature, is practifed, not only with impunity, but with approbation?

---------Quid non mortalia pictora cogis
Auri facra fames------------------------VIRG.

If you think my expreffions of abhorrence too fanguine, let me
advife you to confult the *Hiftoire Philofophique et Politique des E-
tabliffements et du Commerce des Européens dans les deux Indies ;
livre onzieme.* The paffage, though dictated by the profoundeft
wifdom, and animated by the moft refined humanity, is too long
to be recited.

The Doctor imagines, ' that an internal defpotifm may be qua-
' lified and limited; but the defpotifm of one ftate over another has
' no meafure in the exercife of power, but its difcretion.' There
are, however, limits to its vengeance and rapacity, infinitely more
powerful than thofe of arbitrary will. There is a magic in the
voice of intereft, which procures it univerfal audience and refpect.
It would be not only tyranny but madnefs, fhould the rapacity of a
ftate drain the fources from whence alone it can expect the moft
copious and perennial fupplies. It would be blind and implacable
fury, even in beings gratuitoufly wicked, which is not the character
of human nature, to exhauft their rage in one effort, which, by
gradual exertion, might be indefinitely varied and protracted. No
ftate, therefore, however enamoured of **wealth** or **power**, will, by
one

one gluttinous repaſt, devour all the means of future gratification. But, in hiſtory, few examples will be found of one ſtate governing another, except by deputation.

What he obſerves, concerning the difficulty with which one ſtate is emancipated from the tyranny of another, is, in ſome meaſure, yet not abſolutely nor univerſally juſt. It may frequently be more eaſy to diſtract the views, and embroil the intereſts of many tyrants, than to cut off one ; though a ſingle blow, when it can reach him, may prove deciſive of his fate. Beſides, all power is limited by itſelf. Governments, inſatiable of authority and opulence, awake the jealouſy, reſentment, and envy of circumjacent kingdoms ; and only riſe upon the ruins of their neighbours, to accelerate the date, and augment the weight and lumber of their own. But the internal maladies, produced by ſuperfluity and crudity of nutriment, are ſtill more dangerous and fatal. Overgrown ſtates, like overgrown bodies, as they increaſe in corpulency and groſſneſs, become more and more obnoxious to perdition, as well by ſurfeits as by other acute diſeaſes, and grow more cadaverous and abominable, as their appetites are voracious, or their aliment exceſſive. When, therefore, the luſt of conqueſt or of rule prevails in any ſtate, no more than common penetration is neceſſary to foreſee its impending diſſolution.

We are next told, ' That no diſtant country can govern another ' without a military force :' And, to illuſtrate this maxim, a long train of ſuppoſitions are introduced, all of which might be realized, and ſome allowed to be real grievances, if Great Britain and America were proved to be different ſtates ; but, till this be effectuated by more cogent arguments than the Doctor has yet offered, not one of the ſuppoſitions, ſo artfully tagged together, can imply the remoteſt tendency to uſurpation in the Britiſh legiſlature.

Let us, in our turn, ſuppoſe, That, in any diſtant province of the ſame country, for the immediate redreſs of particular exigences, by the tenderneſs of the legiſlature, inferior powers were conſtituted, with conſpicuous and permanent impreſſions of ſubordination to its own. Suppoſe that ſubordination, for a ſeries of years, admitted, and recognized as legal. Suppoſe this province, by its ſituation in the frontiers of the kingdom, and by the real or imaginary value of the commodities which it produces, continually expoſed to hoſtile incurſions and depredations. Suppoſe the nation to which it belongs, on that account, reduced to the diſagreeable alternative, either of reſigning it to her enemies and its own, or of ſupporting its independence and her own right, at the expence of mighty armaments and ineſtimable treaſures. Suppoſe, by theſe interpoſitions, the province ſhould become populous and wealthy. Suppoſe it ſhould then refuſe every acknowledgment to its benefactreſs for former favours, and even pretend, that the advantages ariſing from mutual intercourſe were an ample compenſation. Suppoſe the country ſhould then exert its right of ſupreme controul,

but

but afterwards be feduced by the clamours of inteftine faction, or the remonftrances of the feditious province, to fufpend the efforts of her authority, and only demand a fmall tax upon certain commodities imported, as a recent and manifeft acknowledgment of her fovereign power. Suppofe, likewife, that thefe goods, in the ordinary courfe of trade, were fent; but, before they could be landed, the inhabitants affembled in a tumultuous manner, and in a fury, compared with which the ordinary exhibitions of riot and felony might be termed peace and order, not only infulted the government, but violated the property of a commercial company, by deftroying the merchandize: Was it not high time for fuch a country to vindicate its profaned authority? Could it be expected, that judges, though nominated by the government, yet paid by the province, and refiding in it, would pronounce their fentence with juftice and impartiality? Could it be hoped, that juries, connected with the rioters, nay, perhaps perfonally active in the crime, would give their verdicts againft actions which they themfelves poffibly approved, and delinquents with whom they were allied in the ftricteft manner? Was it, therefore, contrary to any law, that the legiflature fhould interpofe, in fuch a manner, as might fubject the criminals to be tried by perfons who had no intereft in their condemnation, but the dictates of juftice and public fpirit? If perpetrations of this kind are innocent and inculpable, it muft then be granted, that the meafures employed by government were ufurpations; but if, on the contrary, every circumftance which can aggravate the danger and turpitude of political enormities is implied in the conduct which we have now defcribed, thofe who have been guilty of it are rebels and traitors to their Maker, to their brethren of mankind, and to their country, in every fenfe of the words. Let Dr Price, therefore, determine, whether a country, in endeavouring to regain its original rights, may not be animated by nobler principles than criminal ambition, or unjuft refentment.

It is however falfe, that a province thus juftly and publicly ftigmatized can be in the fame ftate as Great Britain, ' were our firft ' executive magiftrate, our Houfe of Lords, and our Judges, no- ' thing but the inftruments of a foreign democratical power; were ' our juries nominated by that power; or were we liable to be ' tranfported to a diftant country, to be tried for offences commit- ' ted here; and reftrained from calling any meetings, confulting ' about any grievances, or affociating for any purpofes, except when ' leave fhould be given us by a Lord-Lieutenant or Viceroy.'

For, let it be remembered, that difcriminating circumftances fubfift in different countries, which have no influence, or at leaft ought to have none, in different provinces of the fame ftate. The fpirit of laws, the coincidence of characters, principles, and interefts which unite the people of one country, may be, and generally are, incompatible with thofe of another. Hence the reduction

duction of one hoftile nation to the laws and government of its conqueror, muft produce the total fubverfion of its religious and civil oeconomy. Hence, every principle of intrinfic motion is entirely annihilated, and new biaffes impreffed by the conquering ftate, which are moft agreeable to its tafte, or conducive to its intereft.

Should Great Britain be tranfported to heaven, of which, however, there feems to be no immediate danger, perhaps our author, in the tendernefs of his patriotic zeal, might imagine the liberties of his country extinct, becaufe it would then be under a foreign adminiftration, whofe power could not poffibly be checked or controlled. But, whenever this diftant revolution fhall happen, I hope there are few of his Majefty's good fubjects who will be difpofed to murmur at the change, or complain, that he is not permitted to fulfil the determinations of his own mind.

It has already been obferved, that the principles of union, conftituent of the fame country, may be fufceptible of minute difcriminations, which neither violate nor deftroy the fyftem, if properly regulated. Some of thefe diverfities take place between Great Britain and her colonies.

The iflands of America, and its northern provinces, have found it convenient and lucrative to carry on an illicit trade with the rivals and enemies of their mother-country, even in a ftate of war, whilft they acknowledged the legitimacy and propriety of thofe acts, which were ratified by the parliament of Britain, relative to navigation and trade. If, then, they were an independent ftat., their procedure was contrary to the faith of nations; if a fubordinate province, it was an infamous infringement of their allegiance to their country.

We know, that fraudulent practices of this kind, by their familiarity, have loft that idea of turpitude and villany with which they ought ever to be attended But dithoneft alienations of the public patrimony, whatever fentiments they may excite, are no lefs criminal and difhonourable in themfelves, but infinitely more pernicious than depradations of private property, which are rewarded with a rope. Will any man, however, affirm, that this collifion of interefts is fufficiently momentous to conftitute the diftinction between one country and another; or that the confequence of reftraining fuch unlawful practices is the lofs of liberty to thofe on whom thefe reftraints were impofed? If fo, all, or moft of the people in England or Scotland, who inhabit the fea-coaft, form certainly a country diftinct from the reft, becaufe the fame views of intereft impel them to carry on the fame prohibited trade; their liberties, therefore, are effectually annihilated, and the officers of cuftoms and excife are, upon this fuppofition, the delegates of tyranny, to hold them in eternal fervitude, and rob them of their lawful acquifitions.

F. It

It was not without indignation of foul, that I read this paſſage in the Doctor's Obſervations, which I ſhall now tranſcribe verbatim : ' Perhaps,' ſays he, ' in ſome caſes, under the pretence of the im-' poſſibility of gaining an impartial trial where government is re-' ſiſted, it will ordain, that offenders ſhall be removed from the ' province to be tried within its own territories : And it may even ' go ſo far, in this kind of policy, as to endeavour to prevent the ef-' fects of diſcontents, by forbidding all meetings and aſſociations ' of the people, except at ſuch times, and for ſuch particular pur-' poſes, as ſhall be permitted them.'

The whole apology which he offers to the public, for that ſyſtem of ſedition propagated by himſelf and his party, is founded upon this glaring falſehood, that Britain and America are different ſtates. Hence we are taught to believe the legitimacy of their reſiſtence. Hence their intrigues and cabals, for concerting and maturing plans of miſchief and deſtruction, are charitably ſoftened, by the milder terms of Meetings and Aſſociations. Hence the juſt convictions of government, that an impartial trial could not poſſibly be gained, where its lawful mandates were reſiſted, are impudently called Pretences. To what civil power, for heaven's ſake, would the Doctor render Britiſh troops amenable ? To the provincial councils and aſſemblies of America, who never could boaſt a civil power but what was transferred to them from their mother-country ? Let the meaneſt Britain explore his own heart, and try whether he can endure ſuch an idea with patience.

Our author now examines the different rights of government which one ſtate may acquire over another, and reſolves them into ' conqueſt, compact, or obligations conferred.' I ſhould only trifle with your patience, and inſult your judgment, were I to purſue him through all theſe unneceſſary diſquiſitions. Let it ſuffice to anſwer, that the relation between different ſtates is by no means the ſame with the relation between a parent-ſtate and its colonies.

In this caſe, beſides the natural principles of union, which we have formerly mentioned as conſtituent of a country, the rights of compact and obligation conjoin their force, to render the political coalition firm and durable ; and while the obligations are inceſſantly repeated, and indiſpenſibly neceſſary for the ſubſiſtence and ſecurity of thoſe on whom they are conferred, it can neither be juſt nor expedient to diſſolve the compact.

The author's poſition may be admitted, that, as it is impoſſible to form a proper eſtimate of civil liberty, ſo no remuneration can atone for its loſs. But if the coloniſts reſign no more than a free conſtitution is intitled to exact from the different parts of its territory, How can ſuch conceſſions be denominated the Loſs of Liberty ? A rebellious province, indeed, may provoke the ſupreme legiſlature to impoſe ſuch reſtraints, or inflict ſuch puniſhments, as are

proper

proper to fecure its authority from prefent dangers, or future inju＊
ries. Thefe reftraints or punifhments may deprive the gu:lty of
perfonal freedom : But this is a precaution neceffary to the general
welfare, and an indifpenfible forfeiture to public juftice. Let no
man deplore the lofs of liberty, who would exert it, if poffeffed, in
working out his own perdition, and that of his fellow-citi＊
zens.

The Doctor juftly informs us, That it would be trifling to apply his
former principles to the government of different ftates contained in
the fame empire. But, he adds, that, in the prefent cafe, fuch an
application is neceffary ; which is faying no more, than that, when
a man has entered on a courfe of fophiftical reafoning, for a particular purpofe, he muft bring it to a fuitable concluiion. To bring
the queftion to a fhort iffue, let a categorical anfwer be demanded
from our author, Whether the characteriftical principles, laws, and
manners of Great Britain and America, be not more identical than
thofe of any other ftates, which are abfolutely diftinct one from
another ? Whether the reciprocation of interefts, between thefe two
regions, be not more palpable and intimate than can poffibly fubfift
in different countries ? And, Whether the interefts of either can
be partially affected, without being, in fome degree, felt by the
whole ?

When he has anfwered thefe queries in the negative, and fhown
that there is no fuch union of principles and interefts, his arguments may be allowed fome efficacy ; but, till then, they can only de-
monftrate the abfurdity of a caufe which depends upon fuch feeble
and ineffectual refources. The Americans and Britains are not different ftates, but the fame in different fituations. Their connections are fuch as muft eftablifh and continue a reciprocation of interefts. Their legiflatures never were independent one of another.
The provincial councils and affemblies derive not only their power,
but their exiftence, from the Britifh legiflature.

With a view to remove a natural objection, he afks, Whether
this empire ought not to have a fovereign legiflature, a controlling
power ? I have formerly fhown, that this is equally effential to
every form of government. What inferior communities are to regal, fuch are kingdoms to imperial ftates. A fenate, therefore,
like what he defcribes page 7. and refumes in the paffage which is
now the fubject of our animadverfion, muft confift in a reprefentation of ftates, as the parliament of Great Britain confifts in a reprefentation of counties and boroughs. It may be obferved of every
free government, that, in proportion as its affairs are fimplified,
they will be more clearly and generally underftood. And, in pro＊
portion as the people can enter into the public neceffities and in-
tentions, when their minds are not diftracted by the interpofitions
of faction, or retarded by the powerful attraction of private intereft,
compliances will be obtained, and enterprizes undertaken with
greater

greater eaſe and chearfulneſs. But, when a government is extenfive, when it involves multiform and ſubordinate juriſdictions, its
rights, in many caſes, become inſcrutable, its powers indefinite,
and its affairs complex and intricate. In all governments, the welfare
of the whole is effectuated and continued by partial and temporary
ſacrifices of private intereſt, to permanent and general advantage.
Theſe conceſſions are as neceſſary to be made by the ſtates which
conſtitute an empire, as by the communities which form a kingdom. Hence we may eaſily conceive, in general, what is meant
by the private concerns of ſtates, and what by the common concerns of the empire. But it will not be ſo eaſy to find an infallible
criterion, an obvious barrier, by which, in every particular in-
ſtance, they may be diſtinguiſhed one from the other. Whilſt, therefore, they continue ſo intimately united, as, in many caſes, to be inextricable, the legiſlation of no particular ſtate can be entirely independent, but muſt, on many occaſions, ne over-ruled by the decrees
of that ſenate, whoſe common concern is the general proſperity of the
empire. So far, therefore, as any particular government is controlled, it muſt be ſubordinate ; and, ſo far as the decrees of the
delegates are recognized and fulfilled, the ſovereignty of the ſenate
is acknowledged. But, ſhould the ſenate finally diſagree in their
opinions, or ſhould the reſults of their deliberation be diſavowed
and reſiſted by the ſtates, the union of the government is deſtroyed,
and a poſture of affairs, analogous to anarchy in kingdoms, takes
place.

PART II. We are now arrived at the ſecond part of our obſervations, in which the author aſſerts, that, from one leading principle,
he has deduced a number of conſequences, that ſeem to him incapable of being diſputed. How far his opinion is right, let your
own reflection and knowledge, let the ſtrictures upon that part of
the work which has already been reviewed, determine your judge-
ment.

We are next informed, that it was his intention to apply all the
arguments formerly urged to the queſtion between Great Britain
and America. This we might have diſcovered without the aſſiſtance of an oracle. But, to remove national prejudices, and reconcile us to the important concluſions which he intends to draw
from this application of his principles, we are liberally favoured with
preliminary reflections, which you may read at your leiſure, without my attendance. For, when examined, they do not appear of
ſuffici-nt importance, either to enlighten your doubts, or to increaſe
your entertainment.

- America may, perhaps, be regarded by the Engliſh as ſubjected
to the individuals of that nation ; but, in Scotland, no ſuch arrogant pretences are indulged We never eſteemed them leſs than
ourſelves; we always thought them, like ourſelves, accountable to
the Britiſh legiſlature, but never to any Britain, nor to any other
power

power under heaven. If the Doctor's countrymen entertain the sentiments with which he charges them, it will be difficult to judge, whether their ignorance is more the object of ridicule, or their ambition, of contempt.

It is, however, no favourable omen for the Doctor, that history, precedents, statutory laws, and arguments drawn from charters, are thought improper mediums for the trial of his cause. Humanity, reason, and justice in public transactions, whatever the author may imagine, have frequently been of sufficient importance to impress upon history, laws, and precedents, a sanction too venerable to be rejected, without reflecting dishonour upon those who appeal to different tribunals. But it seems the origin and increase of our American colonies are new. Is this a reason sufficient to invalidate the judgment formed, and to confront the transactions approved of by our ancestors? If history contains no events exactly similar to the rise and progress of America, Must we likewise imagine that it contains none which are analogous; and, in such cases, may not the sense of nations, as far as the analogy can justly be carried, have sufficient weight with us to determine our opinions, and regulate our conduct? Must we abandon the tracts of political experience, the maturest counsels of statesmen and sages, for the false and chimerical ideas of a liberty which never did, nor ever can possess any existence, but in the brain of fanaticism, or the bombastic ebullitions of a factious imagination.

The author is justly afraid, that this unhappy controversy must now be decided by other weapons than reasoning. He detests the measures which have brought affairs to this inauspicious crisis; but he forgets from what principles these measures were deduced, with what intention they were adopted, and by whom they were pursued. Though Britain first drew the sword, is she for that reason to be judged the aggressor? Is the man in private life, who, in vindication of his rights, anticipates his foe, and draws his sword for self-defence, guilty of a gratuitous assault? There can be no doubt concerning the views entertained by the people of America for a series of years, tho' they have been mean enough to deprecate the wrath of Britain, in the endearing characters of Brethren, Countrymen, and Fellow-subjects. Though they have loudly declared it their ultimate wish to be reinstated in the same situation in which they found themselves posterior to the late peace, it has for a long time been no secret, that they indulged the romantic and extravagant project of asserting their own independence by arms; and, had they suffered this design to remain silent and progressive till mature for execution, who knows where it might have issued? But the results of time and fortune were too slow for the impatience of their heroic genius: Destitute of every internal resource, whether for subsistence or defence, they urge their claim to independence in thunder, and vindicate their liberties by measures too arbitrary to be pursued by the most sanguinary despot without blushes and remorse. From

their humane and civilized neighbours, having borrowed the lau-
dable arts of fighting in ambufcade, and of enumerating the victims
of their valour by the fcalps which they produce ; by thefe means,
they exert their benevolence and delicacy upon the perfons of their
acknowledged brethren, their fellow-fubjects, and their countrymen !

Such is the injuftice of the war at prefent carried on by Great
Britain againft her colonies, and fuch are the caufes for which our
author, in the fpirit of prediction, pronounces it curfed. Dreadful
is the certainty, that, fooner or later, the curfe of God muft attend an
unjuft war; but, on whofe devoted head the vials of omnipotent
wrath fhall defcend, let the fupreme and equitable arbiter of heaven
and earth determine.

Some of thefe obfervations may, perhaps, appear to be infpired
by innate malignity, or perfonal refentment. It may be faid, that,
if fuch invectives have any public influence at all, they can only
be intended to whet the fword, and light the torch for the devafta-
tion and perdition of America. But, you, my friend, who know
the inmoft receffes of my heart, you are amply qualified to vindicate
it from fuch infernal imputations. God, the omniprefent witnefs
and fovereign judge of all, whofe intimate infpection detects the
moft latent purpofes and retired emotions of the human foul, can
teftify for me, that I neither thirft for the blood, nor rejoice in the
calamities of America. On the contrary, if I am at all a judge of
my own fentiments, I fhould efteem it my glory, my felicity, to
reconcile them to their intereft and their duty, by every perfonal
facrifice in my power. But becaufe, as a man and a Britain, I
compaffionate the miferies which they have provoked, muft I likewife become the abettor of their treafons, the apologift of their
crimes ? When the colonies return to a fenfe of duty and fubmiffion, not a Britifh bofom fhall glow with warmer wifhes than mine
to fee the fword of juftice fheathed, and mercy borne on the fwift-
eft wings of angels, flying to diffufe the heavenly mandate of univerfal fafety and happinefs. If the demands of Nemefis muft be
heard, if it fhould be abfolutely neceffary to difplay the terrors of
vindictive power, there are other objects, lefs remote, on whom
the vengeance may defcend with greater propriety. Let England
tear from her own heart the fnakes and vultures which poifon its
tranquillity, and corrode its happinefs. There are domeftic he-
ralds of fedition, living and active firebrands of difcord, in our very
bowels. For them, and not for the infatuated Americans, let the
axe be fharpened, and gibbets rife to heaven.

After informing us what is his defig   and preparing us to relifh
it, the Doctor propofes to profecute it in the following manner.

1. To

1. To inquire what the war with America is, in refpeƈ of ju-
ſtice.

2. The principles of the conſtitution.

3. In refpeƈ of policy and humanity.

4. The honour of the kingdom.

And, *laſtly*, The probability of fucceeding in it.

SECT. 1. In the firſt feƈtion of the fecond part, we are told,
that ' the inquiry, whether the war with the colonies is a juſt war,
' will be beſt determined by ſtating the power over them, which
' it is the end of the war to maintain : And this cannot be better
' done, than in the words of an aƈt of parliament, made on pur-
' pofe to define it.' That aƈt, it is well known, declares, " That
" this kingdom has power, and of right ought to have power, to
" make laws and ſtatutes to bind the colonies, and people in A-
" merica, in all cafes whatever." " Dreadful power indeed," ex-
claims our author, with as much aſtoniſhment, as if he had fud-
denly beheld the head of Medufa, and been petrified with horror
at the fight. But, is this power in reality fo formidable ? has it
been fo oppreſſive to the counties and boroughs of Great Britain ?
yet thefe are communities as different one from another, as the
colonies from them, if we except fuch difcriminations as are merely
local. What then can be meant by all thefe anticipations of terror, which our benevolence infpires for our friends and countrymen, whilſt we forget that we ourfelves live beneath the fame oppreſſive rod, whofe effeƈts appear fo tremenduous in America, without feeling its weight ? In ſhort, if the author admits that the colonies are conneƈted with Great Britain by fimilarity of charaƈter,
by unanimity in their general principles or national fpirit, by political compaƈts, by mutual obligations, and by reciprocation of intereſt, he muſt allow them to conſtitute the fame ſtate ; to be lawfully fubjeƈted to the fame legiſlature ; to be virtually reprefented
in the fame conſtitution ; and, confequently, to poſſefs the fame
degree of freedom with that maternal country, from whence they
derive their form, their genius, and their power.

But, if we believe the Doƈtor, whatever be the limits to which
the Britiſh legiſlature ſhall reduce its claims, if it has any claim at
all, its authority muſt ſtill be boundlefs and indefinite. Men who
think and fpeak rationally of government, muſt indeed acknowledge, that, when extraordinary emergencies occur, uncommon expedients become neceſſary. But, is it for that reafon, probable, or
even poſſible, that a legiſlature ſhould. on every trivial occafion,
exert the plenitude of its power, and effeƈtuate by violence thofe
general purpofes which the univerfal conviƈtion of its right and the
fenfe of public utility, are fufficient to accompliſh ? Can tyranny
be ever eligible to any people for its own fake ? A fingle defpot may
flatter himfelf that his perfonal fecurity and independence, eſſen-

tially require the full exercise of his power. He may gratify his own rapacious or sanguinary difposition, becaufe he is neither controlled by others equal to himfelf in power, nor checked by views extrinfic to his own perfon and its exigences. But the domination of one people over another, (however extenfive its rights), muft employ lefs effectual means, and be circumfcribed by narrower limits, unlefs it fhould rule, as we have obferved above, by delegated fway ; and, in this cafe, a foreign defpot may be worfe than a domeftic tyrant, whofe cruelty and avarice may be foftened by perfonal connections, or amicable prepoffeffions. The exertion of indefinite rights by one people over another can at worft be no more than occafional and temporary, and can only happen, when violent difeafes demand violent remedies. Should Britain attempt to free herfelf from the burden of public debts, by extorting with, violence and inhumanity from her colonies fuch taxes, as are difproportioned to their abilities or refources, in depriving them of the means of commerce, fhe drains the original fountains from whence her future opulence may flow. Thus, her indigence will not only become infupportable, but hopelefs. Are thefe experiments to be tried, even in the moft defperate circumftances, by a people intent upon its fafety, and anxious for its credit? As far then, as the wealth and profperity of Great Britain are dependent upon the wealth and profperity of her colonies, fo fecure are the colonies themfelves from her exorbitant demands, or oppreffive injunctions. This tenor of common fecurity, being founded, not only on political compact, but on the nature of things, muft be more permanent and inviolable, than any one which originates merely in ftatutary laws or temporary charters.

It is acknowledged by our author, that, when the deburfements of America for the common defence were difproportioned to their refources, they were fupplied by a parliamentary grant from Great Britain. Why then has fhe not a right to demand redrefs for exigences of the fame nature, arifing from the fame caufes? But, after all the Doctor's pomp of reafoning, as it terminates in a falfe principle, it is no more than mountains labouring to bring forth mice. For it is falfe, that the people of America are fubjected to thofe of Britain, more than the people of Britain to thofe of America. It is true, that the perfons who conftitute the Britifh legiflature are Britons by birth, by character, by education, and intereft. But thefe circumftances, as I have formerly fhown, do not form a greater diftinction between Britons and Americans, than between people of different counties in Britain. It is true, that they are not chofen by the voices of the people in America ; for which, fee the reafons in a pamphlet called Taxation no Tyranny. But it is equally true, that they are as much the virtual reprefentatives of America, as of all the people in Great Britain, who are not magiftrates, burgeffes, or freeholders.

It is true, that the laws made for America in Great Britain cannot
so immediately and fensibly affect the persons and interests of those
who make them, as these which have force in Britain alone. But, tho'
the effects are not so immediate and fensible, they are not less real
and important. Should the commerce of America remain in lan-
guor or fuspense, the British merchant would quickly and delicately feel the diminution of his resources. He would endeavour to
prevent bankruptcy, if at all avoidable, by retrenching his expences.
These retrenchments must proportionably influence the situations
of the farmer and manufacturer. From thefe the hardship must
soon pass to the landed-interest.

Upon those principles, the absurdity of all wanton extortions
from America will appear in the most glaring light; and it will be
obvious, that the same reasons which constitute the members of
parliament representatives of the people in this island who cannot
vote, must likewise render their representation of America equally
real and legitimate. Both the people, therefore, are subject to the
same legislature; but neither one to the other.

Every free constitution is only susceptible of liberty in a given
proportion. Such people as are neither qualified to vote nor judge,
must be contented with that degree of personal freedom which is
adequate to the powers they possess, and the sphere in which they
act. Even the contingent circumstances of number and distance
have real, but unavoidable effects upon public liberty. Britain, and
all her colonies, feem at present in full possession of all the liberties
of which they are capable, and, indeed, of more than they deserve,
because of more than they know how to use. The Doctor is therefore egregiously mistaken, if he imagines that we offer our own
want of liberty, either as a precedent or consolation for the slavery
of others. It appears, then, that the supreme legislature is neither,
in any peculiar sense, the exclusive legislature of Great Britain, nor
of America, but equally of both.

If, therefore, America be absolutely submitted to its difcretion,
so likewise is Great Britain. If it be self-evident, that the Americans have nothing left which they can call their own, neither have
the Britains. In litigations of property, which fall not within the
jurisdiction of interior courts, neither the Americans nor Britains
are judges, but the legislature alone. When exigences of state demand supplies, the bulk of the people in neither of these regions
can be thought qualified, either to estimate the quantum, or to investigate the best manner in which it may be levied. The powers,
therefore, which are invested in the legislature, both over the Britains and Americans, must be discretionary. But, since we have
seen, that the very persons by whom these demands were made, if
they should prove extorsive and iniquitous, must, in their own for-
tunes, more or less immediately suffer from their bad effects; what
reason can there be to fear that the latitude of this discretion will

F   be

be further extended when applied to America, than when exerted in Great Britain ?

All concretes, which take their denomination from their form, lose their exiſtence with their principles of coheſion. Such is the conſtitution, and ſuch the fate of empires. When the cauſes of their union are ineffectual to preſerve it, the empires are no more, but naturally reſolve into their component parts, which, by that ſolution, are as effectually disjoined as any ſimilar parts through the whole globe can poſſibly be. According to our author, the union of a ſtate eſſentially conſiſts in the unity of its legiſlation. This union in America and Great Britain he denies ; and the principles which he ſubſtitutes, as the cauſes or preſervatives of ſuch an union, are the ſame with thoſe political alliances, or commercial treaties, which may ſubſiſt between any ſtates, and actually do ſubſiſt, without conſtituting any principle of union among them. What he means by ' a common relation to one ſupreme executive head,' I am at a loſs to determine. One thing is certain, that ſuch a relation muſt be inconceiveably frail and precarious.

The family of Stewart felt the crowns of Scotland and England no extremely eligible poſſeſſion, till the union of the kingdoms under one legiſlature reconciled their views and intereſts. Let us ſuppoſe, what might naturally happen, if the councils and aſſemblies of America were ſupreme and independent, that ſome commercial diſpute ſhould occur, in the courſe of negotiations between this iſland and the continent. The legiſlatures, by the ſuppoſition, are each of them ſupreme and independent. Might not each of them expect, from the ſame executive power, ſuch offices and enterprizes as were incompatible ? The royal negative could have no effect in promoting the ends of either nation. The executive magiſtrate, like a ball ſuſpended between two attractions, equal in force, but oppoſite in direction, muſt be incapable of exerting the power with which he was inveſted. Should he interpoſe in a ſecondary manner, and offer his mediation in the diſpute, he deſcends from his executive character, and exchanges it for that of an umpire. Now, I would gladly aſk Dr Price, How agreeable he thinks a manoeuvre of this kind to the nature and genius of practical politics ? How the ſupreme magiſtrate could extricate himſelf, if the nations remained inflexibly tenacious of their purpoſes ; and whether it is poſſible that the common relation, in ſuch circumſtances, could poſſibly ſubſiſt ? But, if the methods of union propoſed by our author are not ſufficient to preſerve the coalition of the Britiſh empire, he fairly conſigns it to deſtruction in the name of God. An important ſentence ſhould be pronounced with proper ſolemnity. ' In the name of God,' ſays he, ' let it want that unity ;' that is to ſay, let it want that principle which alone can conſtitute an empire.

The

The word *superiority*, as employed by the Doctor, is extremely ambiguous. The distinction between moral and political superiority is so clear, and so momentous, that they ought never to be confounded in the present question. Wealth, as the parent of luxury, must, without doubt, in the course of time, corrupt and debase any state. But, whilst the constitution sublists in its integrity, nay, if originally potent, for some time after the commencement of its decline, superior property will produce superior power. To prove this, we need neither enter profoundly into the constitution of our nature, nor into the theory of politics; it is plain from common sense and palpable experience. By what supernatural means our author has acquired the art to estimate the knowledge and virtue of countries, I pretend not to determine. But, since neither artithmetic nor algebra can be applied to quantities of this kind, as to sensible objects, we may be tolerably certain, that the mediums must be different which he employed to calculate the national debt. In both, however, he may well be suspected of inaccuracy; because the data upon which he proceeds are neither easy to be ascertained in the one nor the other.

If the reciprocation of kind affections, of tender tasks, and useful offices between ourselves and those to whom we owe our birth, constitute the parental and filial relation; Why should not the same causes produce analogous effects in the political as in the individual system? When colonies are transplanted, the difficulties under which they labour are generally as insuperable, without the assistance of their native country, as those of children without the assistance of their parents. Unacquainted with the nature of the clime and its products; ignorant of the advantages to be improved, or the inconveniencies to be avoided; unskilled in the art, the manner, the season of cultivating and preparing the materials which nature bestows; embroilled in war, or occupied in negociations with savages; fatigued with clearing lands, or building habitations; the assistance and protection of their maternal state are not only indispensibly necessary to their welfare, but even to their being, till long experience, and repeated instructions, have taught them to investigate and improve the native riches of their new establishment.

These acquisitions are neither quickly nor cheaply to be procured. The gradations of their progress will be slow, as the numbers to be instructed, and the difficulties to be conquered, increase. During this important interim, the necessaries of subsistence and defence must be supplied. Inestimable as these favours are, Do they exact no returns from gratitude and justice? If men, thus accumulated with benefits, can, without iniquity, refuse every acknowledgment, Why might not their country, at their original emigration, have abandoned them to all the rigours of their destiny? Why might she not, with absolute indifference, have let them down the
winds

winds of heaven to prey on fortune ? It cannot be doubted, but that the crisis of political virility will arrive. When arts are acquired, manufactures established, government fixed, and inhabitants multiplied ; in a word, when the colony has wisdom to conduct, property to subsist, and strength to defend itself, then, and not till then, comes the period of its independence ; yet even then it ought not to be claimed with temerity. While the political child retains the features, the character, the taste, the manners, and inclinations of its parent; while their general interests are coincident, one would imagine the youthful offspring should be reluctant and timorous, abruptly to shake off a tuition so faithful and tender. It is certainly agreeable to the analogy of nature, and to the voice of reason, that the authority of political, as well as natural parents, should be relaxed, as their offspring rises to maturity ; but it is by this very relaxation, too far carried, that the child is grown prematurely stubborn. Had Britain continued to assert her original claim, had she from time to time exercised the powers which it gave her, the prodigal would have been more effectually inured to reasonable compliances, and the voice of his maternal necessities might have been heard with reverence and attention. But now, that these rights have been so long silent and torpid, the unnatural offspring flattered themselves, that such claims were either buried in voluntary oblivion, or forfeited by irreversible prescription. Hence, when at last renewed, desuetude gave them the air of innovation. Men seldom chearfully listen to demands which lessen the means of their private gratification, or public consequence.

Thus, rather than recognize an authority which appeared forgetful of its own extent, the Americans assumed the spirit, before they had attained the power of resistance. If Dr Price's argument, from this topic, has any force at all, it must presuppose, that the colonies in America have arrived at a state of political maturity : That they are amply capacitated for independence : That they possess every internal resource of subsistence in time of peace, and of defence in war. Yet, can any thing be more visible, than that their prudence is neither ripe for legislation, nor their manufactures capable of supplying their own demands ; nor their arsenals provided with military stores sufficient to maintain a war ; nor their stock of circulating money and public credit adequate to the exigences of an independent state, embroiled with a powerful and wealthy antagonist.

It were a superfluous and fastidious task, to enumerate the proofs of their indigence and debility in all these respects. One, however, I cannot forbear to mention, because it not only evinces the truth of what has been asserted, but is pregnant with consequences more astonishing and flagitious than words can express. If the Americans are internally sufficient for their own necessities, Why do they imbibe with so much avidity, and propagate with so much exultation, every flying report of promised assistance, from the rivals and enemies of Britain ? Why are the banners of France and Spain often oftentatioufly·difplayed in terrific profpect ? If auxiliaries like thefe would be fo grateful to America, no longer let her pretend that liberty, facred liberty, is the prefent object of her contention, or defpotic power of her fupreme abhorrence. If, without French affiftance, fhe cannot defend herfelf againft her mother-country, by whofe interpofition, under what powerful aufpices, when abandoned by Britain, fhall fhe fecure her independency againft the united force of France and its allies ? Has fhe forgot, that the fame fpirit of univerfal domination, the fame plan of politics which were kindled and projected in the cabinet of Lewis XIV. ftill prevail ? Can they expect to ftipulate for liberty with fuccefs, in oppofition to the fpirit and effence of that government whofe interpofitions were neceffary to their refcue ? Will that force be fufficient to repel the hoftilities of a nation, without whofe intervention it muft have been annihilated ? Let it not be urged, that this is a recent propenfity, the effect of a violent and temporary refentment; for, either the politics of America muft be contemptibly crude and unconcocted, or the confequences of her fuccefs againft Britain, by any conjunctions with France and Spain, muft appear obvioufly and unavoidably productive of the confequences which have now been fpecified.

Such is the punifhment of political, as well as natural parricides. This impious brood, who would not only fhed the blood and tear the bowels of her that produced them, but invoke her implacable and hereditary foes to fhare the Cannibal feaft, fhall become the victims of that facriligeous rage which they infpired and approved.

'But the Englifh came from Germany. Does that give the 'German ftates a right to tax us ?' This is a moft emphatic queftion. It ftrikes home. It is decifive of the controverfy. Whence have our patriots derived fuch profound wifdom ? It would, however, be natural to imagine, that, in retrofpects of this kind, Englifh writers, for the honour of their nation, fhould be more referved and delicate. When we fee their origin deduced from the Germans, it is not eafy to fufpend the excurfions of a petulant imagination, nor to fupprefs the fuggeftions of an officious memory. We cannot forbear to recollect the hiftory of Hengift and Horfa; the reafons for which they were called to Britain; the entertainment which they found; and the manner in which they improved the public hofpitality. We have all along acknowledged, that there is a period in political, as well as in natural life, when colonies owe neither tribute nor fubmiffion to the legiflature of their mother-country. The Englifh are now confiderably diverfified from the Germans in their characters, their manners, their laws, and their interefts. They have been long able to fubfift of themfelves, without any other affiftance or protection from Germany, except fuch as may be expected from one ally to another. Is this the ftate of A-merica ? Unlefs our author and his friends can anfwer this queftion in the affirmative, their arguments drawn from the conduct of Germany towards England, will prove nothing but the imbecility of fuch as propofe or regard them

We muſt now, it ſeems, balance accounts with America; and, for the charge of protection and aſſiſtance which has been ſtated againſt the continent, we are referred to the 13th page of the obſervations, where the rights to be acquired by obligations conferred are conſidered. But though, according to the Doctor, this important article is fully obviated, by the reaſoning contained in that paſſage, he ſtill adds, that the benefits conferred upon the continent, were not on its account, but ours. This he proves from the preamble to an act of parliament. To anticipate the cavils of faction, and the murmurs of ignorance, it is uſual for the legiſlature to introduce its decrees, with an account of their utility or expediency : But, unleſs the Doctor can ſhow that the reaſons aſſigned in the preamble were the genuine intent, the only motives of the act, his quotation will contribute little to his deſign. But, whatever motives produced the benefits beſtowed on America, the benefits themſelves were no leſs ſubſtantial and important ; and, from whatever diſpoſitions they flowed, they conſtitute a civil claim to adequate returns. The Doctor's manner of ſtating articles is more convenient for his purpoſe than expreſſive of his equity. He tells us that, by taking our manufactures at our own price, and by indulging us with the advantages of an excluſive trade, the Americans have conſiderably aſſiſted in ſupplying our poor, paying our taxes, and relieving our debts. On this occaſion, who can forbear to retort his own argument ? If theſe conceſſions to Britain were either the neceſſary reſults of their conſtitution and ſituation, or granted more upon their account than ours, which may be proved even to demonſtration ; why ſhould theſe circumſtances be enumerated to exaggerate the obligations due by Britain, whilſt no deduction is made for more important favours, though they ſhould be granted to flow from motives equally intereſted ? Why are no deductions made in favour of the mother-country ? To ſuch miſerable ſhifts muſt authors be reduced who indiſcriminately undertake all the dirty jobs of a party. Our author tells us, in general, that the Americans contributed much to our ſucceſs in war. But, leſt he ſhould be thought too ſanguinely to urge the cauſe of his clients, he modeſtly avoids all detail. A recapitulation of particulars might have perplexed him. What a beautiful ſtarry night, ſaid a boy to his mother ; the mother looked, and could ſcarcely diſcern a ſingle ſtar in the whole hemiſphere !

‘ But, when aſked in the character of freemen, the Americans ‘ have ſeldom refuſed to gratify our demands.’ By the word ‘ ſel‘ dom’, it ſeems to be inſinuated, that they have denied, or wiſhed to deny requiſitions of this kind, though their favourite mode of taxation. But, in what character, for heaven's ſake, are they now taxed ? If as freemen, why is compliance refuſed ? If as ſlaves, becauſe not actually repreſented, how are the Britains, who are in ſimilar circumſtances, free ?

What

Whatever Dr Price may think of rights to property in land, when emigrations from the different parts of Europe were fashionable, nothing was more usual among those navigators, when they landed, whether on an island or a continent, which was either entirely vacant, or inhabited by savages, than to give a new name to the place, and to fix a pole in the ground, with an inscription, by which it was appropriated to the country from whence they came. Frivolous and childish as this manner of acquiring rights may appear to us at present, it was then allowed, not only to be proper, but sufficient for that purpose. If the Doctor will take the trouble to peruse what has been said by those who are most profoundly skilled in natural jurisprudence, he will find, that property is originally obtained either by donation, by purchase, by excambion, by labour, or by prior occupation. Rights of the last kind are universally allowed to be valid; and, when confirmed by time and possession, they are not only acknowledged by the law of nature and nations, but recognized and ratified, in the positive institutions almost of every civilized country under heaven. Had feudal tenures been extended to America, and continued in exercise for a succession of centuries, would it not have been thought absurd, after that period, to litigate the rights of the superior? Would not the course of time, the fact of possession, the habits and inclinations of the parties concerned, have been deemed sufficient to establish such a right, independent of any other cause? Continued possession, and confirmed habit, are, even among civilians, allowed to have no inconsiderable force in determining property. If, therefore, Britain acquired a right to her American territories by legal means; if her present claim is corroborated by habit and possession, the present aera is too late to call it in question. It may be urged, that the right of the colonists is founded upon purchase, possession, and habit. Still, however, if the right of the original country be prior, it is more valid, and every subsequent claim derived and subordinate. This, however, is another of the topics in which it might have been wished that the Doctor had entered with more reserve. Were the transactions, by which the original constituents of the colonies purchased lands from the natives, uniformly fair and generous? Were their deburfements always equivalent to their acquisitions? Was their conduct free from violence or artifice? Till these questions can be answered with ingenuity, it may perhaps be proper to treat concerning the rights of individuals in America with caution and diffidence.

It is happy for the Doctor that he ' lays no stress upon charters, ' though granted them by an authority which, at the time, was ' thought competent, and rendered sacred by an acquiescence on ' our part for more than one century.' Such charters would have proved but feeble auxiliaries; and he is conscious of their insignificance; not because instruments of public faith, duly and formally
ratified

ratified by all the parties concerned, have no power to render ftipū¬ lations valid and obligatory ; but becaufe they do not contain what he afferts. They do not convey the powers of independent and fo¬ vereign legiflation, nor promife all the colónies immunity from taxation by external authority. Indeed, it is impoffible for a pu¬ blic deed or inftrument to convey the fupreme power of legiflation ; for this would be fuppofing a caufe capable of communicating its own full energy to its effect, and of beftowing priviléges which it could not by any means, nor in any circumftances, retract. Yet, if the Doctor does not think charters binding, to what purpofe, in turbulent feafons, are thofe loud and frequent appeals to the great paladium of our ftate, the Magna Charta ? This is a number of conceffions, extorted by force of arms, from a tyrant, whofe foul was as weak as his fortune was defperate. Yet it is extolled as the great bulwark of Englifh liberty.

The fallacy by which our author attempts to elude the force of that argument which proves America to be as effectually reprefent¬ ed as the greateft number of people in this ifland, has been already detected. If a reprefentation muft be termed defective, becaufe only extended to fuch as are capable of chufing reprefentatives, the fame argument will conclude every reprefentation defective, where every individual is not perfonally reprefented. But inftitutions, which are as perfect as their nature will admit, and their ends re¬ quire, can never be pronounced deficient. There can be no doubt, that, if the Americans fhould, with difinterefted views, and in a proper manner, fuggeft any real and fenfible improvement in our conftitution, fuch an overture might command all the attention which it could deferve. But analyfis or defcription will not be readily efteemed the beft means of improving a political fyftem.

It would not only be unneceffary, but difagreeable, to reiterate the arguments by which we have endeavoured to prove the legal reprefentation of America. If aids extorted from her to relieve Great Britain be wanton or exorbitant, we have formerly fhown that they muft be paid by herfelf, in a manner more difagreeable and hurtful than when immediately difburfed by parliamentary authority. If laws which are made in Britain for America do not iffue in her general or ultimate advantage, the mifchiefs which they produce muft recoil with double vengeance upon the nation where they were made, and the legiflature by which they were enacted. Why then are fuch pueril fophifms, fuch confummate jargon, e¬ ternally bellowed in our ears, which have already been as often refuted as propofed ?

We are now to follow the Doctor in his additional confiderations ; and the firft of thefe is, ‘ Whether, if we have now this fuprema¬ ‘ cy,’ (this fovereign power to taxation and legiflation), ‘ we fhall ‘ not be equally intitled to it in any future time ?’ To demon¬ ftrate the abfurdity of this fuppofition, he mentions the rapidity of
their

their population, the extent of their property, and the succefs of their efforts in arts and fciences. From thefe premifes, he concludes, that, in fifty or fixty years, every particular province may e-qual or furpafs Great Britain. At that period, according to him, if it is unreafonable to fuppofe a people governed by ano-ther, every way fo much their inferior, why fhould it be rea-fonable to govern them at prefent? He defires us, 'to draw the line if we can;' but natur·, tenacious and fucceſsful in all her purpofes, will fave us the trouble. She herfelf has drawn the line, and marked the aera, with fignatures no lefs confpicuous and le-gible than thofe which mark the time when children are entran-chifed from the abfolute dominion of their parents. When colo-nies are mature in the arts of government and legiflation, when they become able to provide for their fubfiftence, and afcer-tain their fecurity, it is equally iniquitous and impoffible, in the nature of things, that their dependence fhould be protracted. But, even by the conceffion of their advocates, the crifis of their eman-cipation is not yet arrived.

Nor is it either neceffary or practicable, that the colonies fhould purfue our government through all its viciflitudes, or participate the evils to which it is obnoxious in every period of its decline, un-lefs the fame caufes which operated in Britain fhould likewife ex-tend their baneful and malignant influence to America. The gra-dations by which a falling ſtate approaches to diffolution, are too plainly difcernible to be miſtaken: And, when this public degene-racy becomes vifible, the colonies, if not infected by the fame mortal difeafe, will not only have fufficient prefcience to perceive their danger, but fufficient fpirit and energy to affert their inde-pendence, and vindicate their liberty.

We have already afferted the difcretionary power of the legifla-ture, both over Britain and her colonies, upon principles which ap-pear to be founded on the nature of things. Indeed, when a legi-flature is formally conftituted, it is abfurd and ridiculous to fup-pofe any particular number of men, impowered by that conftitution, to enact laws which their fucceffors, invefted with the fame powers, cannot repeal. It muſt be acknowledged, that there are laws eter-nal, immutable, and inviolable, by any human decree. Thefe, however, are prior to all particular forms of government. They are coeval with the fupreme lawgiver. They are the inftitutions of God and nature. But thefe are the only barriers which can li-mit the difcretion of any human legiflature. The freedom of any civil government confifts in the undifturbed poffeffion, and free ex-ercife of fuch powers as are fuitable to its neceflities, and adequate to its importance. From the judicious diftribution of thefe powers, and their proper exertion, refult the integrity of the legiflature, and the happinefs of the fubjects. By what infatuation, therefore, will a legiflature be induced to transfer to one branch, a dangerous branch

G   of

of itself, such powers as are equally due to the whole? But, it is said the regal authority has been rendered despotic over Canada, and the same thing attempted in Massachusett's Bay. Whoever will peruse the acts of parliament relative to Canada, must be convinced that the powers invested in his Majesty by these statutes, are merely executive. But executive powers can never be despotic, unless inseparably united with the power of legislation. I cannot forbear to take this opportunity of observing the spirit and conduct which at present so eminently distinguish our august and venerable patriots. Who can be more sublime or diffuse than they in their flaming panegyrics upon the spirit and principles of their native constitution? Who can more warmly enumerate, amongst their most valuable blessings, that liberty and toleration by which their civil and ecclesiastical polity are characterised? Yet, how intensely were these liberal and tolerating spirits kindled by that unpopular act of parliament called the Quebec bill? The inexpiable sin of permitting and authorising the exercise of popery in any part of the British dominions, has been exaggerated with a fury and clamour, equally disgraceful to the British constitution, and the human species. The cession of Canada by France to Britain, is a recent event. All its European inhabitants had been bred in the faith and principles of the Roman catholic church. Were, then, the inhabitants of that northern continent to be expelled from their settlements, or persecuted with fire and sword, upon its accession to the British dominions? Were they not rather to be indulged in the free use of their principles, till they should become the proselites of truth and reason, which could scarcely fail to happen, where Evangelical light is universally diffused, without being intercepted by the interpositions of secular power or policy? I know the intriguing and sanguinary spirit of that religion; the precautions, therefore, taken by our legislature at home, to limit its power and influence, (as necessary for the preservation of public peace and order,) were highly laudable. But, what reason can be urged for extending the same restraints to a distant province, inhabited by papists? If this be English toleration, it is still imperfect, till supported by inquisitors, and instruments of torture. In vain are the military preparations and hostile enterprises against Massachusett's bay represented as acts of tyranny. The inhabitants of that province have no claim to any civil right under heaven. Their effects, their lives, their reputations, are forfeitures to public justice. Humanity will still feel for the sufferings of men, when intense in their degree, and long in their continuance; but their conduct has now rendered it impossible for the most despotic and arbitrary power to treat them with tyranny.

By an unseasonal le and impotent resistence, every claim to be derived from government is lost. For their violation of the political compact is not merely personal; it extends to the whole system of which they

they are members, and tends in some degree to affect the general order of the world. For this reason, it is not sufficient that we use all the positive rights derived from any civil constitution, but even those primary rights which were originally inherent in our nature, the right of exerting our powers, of possessing our effects, of defending our characters, and even of retaining our lives. Whatever exemption, therefore, the province in question may find from any or all of these calamities, must not be attributed to any right which they either at present possess, or can for the future resume, but to unavoidable accident, or to royal clemency alone. Let us not then be told of our injustice, in re-modulating a government, which, after the treason of its subjects, was no longer existent. There is, doubtless, a natural possibility, that one state may subject another to arbitrary power; but Dr Price must be delicately apprehensive, if he imagines, that a government, which is free and jealous of its least important privileges, will put in the hands of its chief magistrate the means of subduing and retaining itself beneath the pressure of irresistible power. The act for regulating the affairs of Quebec, has been so frequently and so insidiously mentioned by the Doctor; it is a topic so inflammatory in itself, that even apostolic charity cannot vindicate such a conduct from malignity of attention. He must either have a bad understanding, or a corrupted heart, who cannot perceive the distinction between obtruding a new religion upon any province, and confirming one which has been already established. What would these declaimers have wished the parliament to do? Must the consciences of the people be forced? must their understandings, misled or prepossessed as they are, be annihilated? Must protestantism convince their minds by military logic? or must they enjoy their religion by connivance? which is infinitely more pernicious and dangerous than the most flagrant violation, or audacious contempt of law. Ye tolerating spirits! ye patrons of justice and liberty! reconcile your conduct with your pretences, if you can; if you cannot, throw off the mask, and discover yourselves to be the disturbers of earth, and the agents of hell! The Doctor supposes his countrymen mighty profuse of their hearts blood; but, in fact, there is no people under heaven who value their own hearts blood more, or that of their neighbours less. Have they not ridiculed the French for their attachment to dramatic probability, and a bloodless theatre? Are they not enraptured with tragedies in proportion to the slaughters which they exhibit? Can any thing more strongly attest their innate love of carnage than the entertainments of the cock-pit, of bear-beating, bull-beating, &c. of which they are so passionately fond?

SECT. II. We now proceed, with our author, ' to examine the ' war with the colonies by the principles of the constitution.' He roundly tells thofe who affirm that we are maintaining the conftitution in America, ' that what they affert is not true; nor, if it ' were, would it be right.' But, I muft be permitted to afk him, Whether it was the defign of the Britifh legiflature, that the governments of America fhould be independent and unaccountable? If fo, why did it referve to itfelf the indefinite and unalienable power of negation? and why was this power recognized in America? It was not limited in its extent to fuch determinations as were of common concern. Can any thing, then, be more obvious, than that, both according to the fenfe of Britain and America, the governments of the colonies were dependent and fubordinate? But, if dependent, they muft be parts of that maternal conftitution to which they owe their origin and fubfiftence. What innovation is then introduced; what charters infringed? Or, if they were infringed, what injury has been done, fince, in the Doctor's opinion, their obligations are fo feeble? It is grofs abfurdity to argue, when it ferves a particular purpofe, from topics, as if they were of the higheft importance, which, at other times, are allowed to be trivial and infignificant.

Our author, however, declares it as his principal intention, to make the following obfervations: ' The fundamental principle of ' our government is, the right of a people to give and grant their ' own money. It is of no confequence, in this cafe, whether we ' enjoy this right in a proper manner or not. Moft certainly we ' do not. It is, however, the principle on which our government, ' as a free government, is founded. The fpirit of the conftitution ' gives it us: And, however imperfectly enjoyed, we glory in it ' as our firft and greateft blefling.'

Any man who is born in a particular country, or who, after his arrival in it, continues to claim its protection, to adapt its manners and cuftoms, to obey and approve its laws, to enter into its interefts and concerns, is effectually engaged in the political compact; becaufe his confent, though never verbally expreffed, is unqueftionably and fufficiently implied in his conduct. As the protection of individuals, and the public fecurity, reciprocally depend one upon another; and, as the public fafety can neither be procured nor afcertained, without public funds, it is the indifpenfible duty and real intereft of every member in a civil fociety, to contribute to thefe funds in proportion to the advantages derived from the conftitution which requires them. In what fenfe, therefore, fubfidies of this kind can be denominated free gifts, I am at a lofs to difcover. Taxes muft always be levied in proportion to the exigences of the ftate, and the abilities of its members. It frequently happens, that neither the quantum nor the quando are arbitrary. Emergencies may occur, in which both the quantity granted, and the feafon when it ought to be raifed, are neceffarily prefcribed by the fame events which create the demand. The right, therefore, of a ftate

to

to require aids in a given quantity, and at a certain period, is abfolute and incontrovertible. How, therefore, any right can fubfift in individuals, to grant or with-hold fuch contributions, muft appear a moft inexplicable myftery. The legiflature, indeed, is the ultimate judge to how much particular fubfidies fhould amount, or by what proportions, and from what fources, they ought to be drawn. But this is as much the duty as the privilege of a legiflature. Upon this right, however, in our author's judgment, the effence of our government depends From this flow our liberty and independence; and, though but imperfectly enjoyed, we glory in it as our moft valuable blefling, becaufe it is the fpirit of the conftitution. Is, then, the fpirit of the conftitution effentially derived from this right? and is the right itfelf imperfectly enjoyed? Gloomy difcovery! Miferable fituation!· The fpirit of our conftitution is then fallacious, and our fenfe of liberty delufive. But, on the contrary, I maintain, that we enjoy this right in a manner as full and perfect as it is practicable for a great and numerous people to enjoy it. Who will affirm, that all the members of an extenfive and populous realm, can either be judges of the time, the manner, or the quantity, neceffary to fupply the demands of government? Who will pretend, that all the members of a ftate are either fufficiently enlightened to chufe reprefentatives, or can be reprefented by perfons of their own election? Yet, as virtual reprefentation extends to the whole community, the principle of political freedom ftill fubfifts, and operates with full vigour, tho' all the individuals do not uniformly act agreeably to the immediate determinations of their will. It is then a grofs and palpable falfehood, that the war is intended to introduce a new conftitut on into America. It is a deplorable, but neceffary expedient, for the reftoration of fafety, order, and peace. We have already feen what a ftrong and fenfible reciprocation of interefts is produced by commerce between Britain and America. From this fingle principle, it will appear, that, by enormous demands upon the colonies, the Britifh conftitution muft quickly bleed itfelf to death. She muft exhauft the fources of vital moifture, prevent its regular circulation, and debilitate all the functions of the ftate. This would not only be to give the King our own money, in giving him theirs; but, like the fpoufe of Hercules, to prefent him with a gift fuperfive of his own power, and deftructive to the ftate which he governs.

SECT. III. Having examined how far the war with America is compatible with juftice, and with the principles of the Britifh conftitution, our author proceeds to confider its ' policy or expe-' diency.' To fhow how impolitical fuch meafures muft prove, he recapitulates the advantages which have accrued to Britain from her connection and intercourfe with the colonies. He enumerates the happy confequences which pacific meafures might have produc',
and

and the pernicious effects of a contrary procedure. He imputes the war to ambition, refentment, avarice, and pride. But here, inftead of concife argument and conclufive reafoning, we are enter-tained with unmeaning rhapfody and declamation. \ u cannot, therefore, expect that I fhould keep him fo clofely in *u v as has hitherto been done. Admitting all the advantageous of hurtful confequences which form his detail to be real and unavoidable, the confideration of a fingle fact deftroys his fine hypothefis, and ex-pofes his arguments to ridicule and contempt The late conduct of adminiftration did not, as has been afferted, infpire the difcon-tents of America, but merely afforded her an opportunity of exprel-fing them.

Nor was the jealoufy of government groundlefs The projected independence of America has long been no fubject of conjecture. Every mind was impreffed with that idea, not from notions or an-ticipations of what might happen, but from the general fenfe of the people, as far as it could be underftood and authenticated by the common intercourfe of life. It is notorious that America, like a charged cannon, lay impregnated with latent mifchiefs, and pre-pared for inftant explofion, when the match fhould be applied. This event, whenever it happened, muft, upon the Doctor's own principles, have blafted every happy confequence which he prefages, and produced every public cataftrophe which he apprehends. It fhould therefore be efteemed a lucky circumftance for this ifland, that America has been fo premature in her declarations, and dif-covered her views before fhe was in a fituation to render them ef-fectual.

Britain, it is faid, can only maintain her fupremacy over Ame-rica, either becaufe it is eligible for itfelf, or becaufe it is connected with fome other public intereft. If maintained for its own fake, its motive muft be the defire of extended dominion, or the luft of power. When authority is violently ufurped, or unjuftly acquired, it cannot be maintained but by criminal ambition. It is, however, quite otherwife when a nation afferts her original and acknowledged rights : In fuch a cafe, the means which fhe employs, though vio-lent, may be juft ; and the legiflature is unworthy of the confidence repofed in it by the public, if it purfues not every method for re-covering the rights, and reftoring the integrity of the ftate. Is this ambition ? Patriots call it fo ; and patriots muft be honourable men! If the arguments formerly ufed by our author be not abfolutely de-cifive of the queftion in agitation, it is beneath the human charac-ter, it is incompatible with the Chriftian temper and profeffion, to deduce the war from any motives but fuch as are worthy and lau-dable. But, fhould a clergyman become the parafite of a party, fhould he exert talents confecrated to the glory of his Maker, and the utility of his fpecies, in diffeminating falfe opinions, and in-flaming popular prejudices? What degree of infamy, already known, is fufficient to brand fuch unpractifed, fuch unprecedented enormities?

We are now prefented with reafons, to prove that the prefent conteft is a conteft for power; and the only one urged is the love of power inherent in our nature, of which the fubfequent arguments are only fo many modifications. But, Is there no other principle inherent in our nature except the love of power? Have we no innate propenfity, no original predilection for juftice? If we have, Why fhould the firft of thefe be the motive of the American war, rather than the laft? When it is objected, that the refiftance of the colonies is likewife a ftruggle for dominion, the Doctor replies, ' That ' it is for felf-dominion, the nobleft of all bleffings.' But will he likewife have the effrontry to affert, that this principle of outarchy is underived and inherent in the conftitution of America? From the powers referved to itfelf by the Britifh legiflature, and from the acquiefcence of America in its determinations, we have fhown, that fuch a principle was neither poffeffed nor arrogated by the colonifts. The Americans, if the Doctor pleafes, have done us no perfonal injury, nor is our vengeance perfonal. But they have injured that republic of which we are members. They have refufed thofe aids which the common exigences required. For, let it be obferved, that, if the government of America be not independent, but really a part of the Britifh conftitution, as I have attempted to fhow, the national debt, which our author difplays and exaggerates with fo much induftry, is, on a double account, no more the debt of England than of America. It is equally due by both, becaufe their conftitution is the fame. It is peculiarly due by America, becaufe much of it was contracted for the defence of the continent.

It is of no moment, in the prefent difpute, whether a revenue from America be the object of government or not. It is of as little importance whether the American trade be of confequence. A people who fuffer themfelves to be cajolled or bullied out of any right, may, with the fame equanimity and refignation, refolve to give up every right. Had America been permitted to dilacerate the empire with impunity, Why fhould not the Ifle of Man likewife affert its independence? Why fhould not Wales be feparated once more from England? Why fhould not Scotland refume its priftine glory?

It is pretended, that the conqueft of America will yield us no advantage. This might have been true, if no rupture had happened between Britain and her colonies. War would then have been diabolical cruelty, and victory itfelf the loweft infamy. But, fince a feparation has been attempted, the colonifts muft either be ours, or have no exiftence at all. For, is it poffible to reflect without perceiving, that, whatever we lofe on the continent, muft become a real and important acceffion of wealth and power to our rivals and our enemies. America is now rendered unanimous by its common danger: Let that but ceafe, and its councils will be immediately diftracted by emulation. A ftruggle for dominion amongft the provinces will enfue. While thus convulfed and fermented by inteftine quarrels, Can it be imagined that the other powers of Europe will remain idle and indifferent fpectators of the conflict? Will they not interfere? Will they not affift the prevailing power; or, by favouring each in its turn, will they not fan the flames of civil diffention, till, by mutual rencounters one with another, the provinces are impoverifhed, and their numbers exhaufted? Thus, their conqueft will be rendered eafy, their fervitude oppreffive, and their fubjection eternal. Thefe, in the common courfe of things, are the moft rational events which can be prognofticated from the abortion of our continental enterprizes. And I now leave you to judge, whether their fuccefs be not effential to the happinefs of America, and highly advantageous to Britain. Let us not flatter ourfelves; political power, like mechanical motion, is never annihilated. It efcapes not from one hand, but by being transferred to another; and, whatever Britain lofes, France or Spain will acquire.

The difference between *meum* and *tuum*, while men are men, has always excited, and will always excite the moft powerful principles of action in their nature. It is an injury no lefs fenfible, to refufe a people what is their due, than to rob them of what they really poffefs. How then can it be furprifing, that fuch ouvert acts of injuftice fhould provoke the warmeft refentment? But it feems ' the ' Americans have fent no military force againft us. They do not ' crofs the Atlantic to extort from us the fruits of our labour.' What a noble effort of felf-denial! What a meritorious exhibition of abftinence! They forbear to wage offenfive war with a foe for whom they tremble, even in their own diftant world, as their patrons affect to call it. But, were they difpofed for fuch a martial expedition, it might be afked, What motive could impel them? How could they be enriched by the fruits of our labour? In its climate, in its foil, and in all the opulence of nature, the region which they inhabit is as much fuperior to England, as England to Lapland or Siberia. Let thofe gentlemen who fo politely and liberally compliment the Scots on the natural difadvantages of their country, confider this, and curfe that littlenefs of foul which can vilely defcend to fuch mean revenge.

Our author charitably imagines, that fome who approve the war, may be actuated by other principles than pride, ambition, or refentment. They may be animated by a zeal for maintaining authority, and for preferving ' the unity or indivifibility of the Britifh ' empire.' I have entered with him into the inquiry contained in the firft part of his pamphlet; I have purfued him through every capital argument. Thefe have been fairly ftated, and, I hope, effec-

tually

tually refuted. It has likewise been shown, that the present measures of government, severe and violent as they may seem, were the only means left us by America, for pursuing and ascertaining those very benefits and advantages which she now pretends to vindicate from the tyranny and rapacity of Britain.

Authority, when its claims are unjust, or its administration weak, has good reason to shun the light of heaven. Impartial discussion and free examination may shake such evanescent fabrics to their foundation. But an authority like that of the British legislature in America, can have no reason for flying to reserve and silence for safety. Claims, derived from reason and equity, may be securely exposed to the view of heaven and earth.

The jealousy of America, entertained by our governors, was not indeed inspired by any public determinations of the continent. nor suggested by any ideas, as the Doctor would injuriously insinuate, that the yoke imposed upon that people was too oppressive to be borne. It was inspired by the prevailing sentiments of the colonies, which, though not in a public capacity, had long been repeatedly and openly declared. The policy so highly extolled by the Doctor, was pursued till it became neither seasonable nor effectual. *Parcere subjectis, et debellare superbos*, is a maxim of state approved by the wisdom, and confirmed by the experience of ages.

We are now regaled with a sanguine detail of enormous blunders in policy, which it would be unnecessary for me to recapitulate. I am no ministerial knight-errant; nor is it either my interest or inclination to defend implicitly the procedure of government in every step. In reviewing this part of the pamphlet, you will find it the Doctor's opinion, that the object of administration was to draw a revenue from America by parliamentary taxation. But formerly, when he thought it necessary to throw an odium upon government, by deducing its procedure from the lust of power, he seems to think, that a revenue from America was not its object, nor the continental trade of much consequence. Such are the subterfuges to which we are reduced, when we mean to carry our point at every expence.

I have already said, that it was neither my business nor concern implicitly to vindicate the transactions of Britain with America. Statutes enacted and repealed, measures pursued and retracted, are certainly politics unworthy of a nation of philosophers, as they are called by the Abbé Renal. The courtier will ascribe them to caution and lenity. By the patriot they will be imputed to the power and interpositions of faction, which alternately revived the spirit of despotism, after it had given way to the remonstrances of sober wisdom. Neither of these opinions may, perhaps, be entirely groundless; but there are other reasons, of a nature more profound, and less conspicuous to general observation, which will always render the government of Britain irresolute and tardy in its

H   interpositions,

interpofitions, when any critical or unexpected emergency occurs. A confiderable body of militia has always infpired the adminiftration with jealoufy, left it fhould too much increafe the power and influence of the people. A ftanding army, depending on the crown for its exiftence and its pay, has always been fufpected, and obnoxious to the people. Hence, in peace, the veteran foldiers, who, by a fucceffion of fevere campaigns, had been inured to courage and difcipline, are difbanded, and left to the miferable alternative of fighting under a foreign banner againft their country, or of procuring a wretched and precarious fubfiftence by robbery at home, which is no longer to be acquired from fuch mechanical labours as they have either never learned, or entirely forgot. Upon the approach of a war, the nation is reduced to the miferable neceffity of collecting a tumultuary and undifciplined force, which, by a profufe expence of blood, and a fevere fucceffion of abortive and difhonourable experiments, muft firft be trained till they become ufeful, and then difbanded.

Confcious of thefe circumftances, Is it poffible for a government to act with vigour and refolution? Can a legiflature boldly determine, what it knows the executive power, entirely difarmed and without refource, muft feel itfelf incapable to perform? Ye minifters of ftate, you who fit at the helm of affairs, with whom are entrufted the glory and happinefs of nations, for once, if, in your department fuch a conduct be practicable, for once be wife, be liberal, be magnanimous! Let the people be empowered and authorifed to defend themfelves. Let them be conftituted, by public authority, the protectors of their own effential interefts. They will be more zealous in performing that duty, than any mercenary butchers of their fpecies whom you can employ. They will be at hand in every impending danger. They will guard, with incorruptible fidelity, whatever is dear to themfelves, or whatever ought to be dear to you, if your confcience can vindicate your procedure to God and them.

Here, whatever confequences may attend the free effufion of my pregnant foul, let me give way to its grief and indignation. When all the troops that could be collected in this realm, or hired from others, are employed in diftant, though neceffary fervice, Why is the unhappy kingdom of Scotland left naked and defencelefs to every invafion? England is already provided with an internal force, which may repel any inconfiderable attack; but Scotland, through its whole extent, is open to the ravage and barbarity of the weakeft and moft defpicable aggreffor. Why are not her own brave and faithful offspring, at leaft permitted to fhed their blood for her glory and fafety? And why, good God! that I fhould live to fpeak it, why was a meafure, fo falutary to both thefe kingdoms, fhamefully and grofsly oppofed in the Britifh Houfe of Commons? Ye inhabitants of England, ye fons of brutality and ignorance, Has God at laft, in juftice, curfed you with judicial and incurable
blindnefs!

blindnefs! Could you not fee, that whoever injures or infults the
kingdom of Scotland, effentially injures and infults yourfelves?
Could you not perceive, that, when fhe is violated, you are expofed ?

Tunc tua res agitur paries cum proximus ardet.

Hor.

But of this enough.

The topics of popular difcontent, upon which patriotifm had
formerly expatiated with fo much triumph and felf-congratulation,
are not ftill thought fufficient to inflame the paffions, and pervert
the judgments of an impetuous and unreflecting people. We muft
now contraft the prefent ftate of affairs with what it was under fome
preceeding reigns. To all this laboured and florid detail, we need
only reply by a few queftions. Whether did the power of legiflation, exercifed in America, originate in Great Britain, or on the
continent ? Whether were its limitations voluntary acts of American liberality, or juft demands of Great Britain, and neceffary
meafures for the welfare of the colonies ? Whether did America offer
any commercial conceffion to Great Britain, which it was confiftent
with her general intereft to refufe ? Whether was not her acquiefcence
in thefe political and commercial regulations, a fufficient indication
of her confent, and, confequently, a fufficient reafon for their eftablifhment ? If thefe were neceffary when the colonies were in their
minority, What reafon could then have been given for eftablifh-
ing and exercifing that form of government, which may not ftill be
given for continuing them ?

In recapitulating the advantages we have loft, the Doctor informs us, that, had we yielded the colonies every unjuft and extravagant conceffion which they demanded ;-had we fuffered them
to remain the nominal fubjects of the Britifh government, they
would not only have allowed us, with pleafure, the reafonable pro-
fits of a continued commerce, but alfo the honour and expence of
defending them, both againft themfelves and their enemies. Had
we felected ~~d purfued thefe meafures, What halcyon days fhould
we have feen ? Plenty would then have anticipated our wifhes, and
honour and dignity courted our acceptance. It is no wonder, therefore, that a conftant and zealous well-wifher of the government under which he lives, fhould call its policy vile, and its exercife a
fcourge, when it adopts fuch meafures as his infcrutable wifdom

long their fixed intention to effectuate, we may fafely affirm, that, for ages of ages, this ifland might have furnifhed them all the manufactures they wanted, without caufing a vacancy in any other department.

What follows, in this fection, is an account of the dangers with which we are threatened, from the uncertain and fluctuating ftate of public credit, and of the tendency which our rupture with America may have to accelerate the ruin we prefage. The whole fuperftructure of Dr Price's reafoning is founded on two fallacies in fact. For, firft, he prefuppofes, that the American governments, though fimilar to ours, are independent of it. And, again, That the Americans would have been contented with their fubjection and dependency, had we not urged them, by the fenfe of its increafing weight, to hazard the moft defperate means of redrefs. It has already been evinced, that the American governments could not poffibly be ignorant of their dependency ; nay, that, virtually, they acknowledged and approved it. It is equally certain, notwithftanding their public acquiefcence, that, for a fucceffion of years, they have entertained views of detachment from the Britifh government. Had the courfe of things proceeded in its former train ; had their progrefs in population, arts, and commerce, met with nothing to interrupt or difconcert it, perhaps the aera of its infranchifement might have been at no great diftance.* To whatever fhocks public credit may be obnoxious, from the prefent pofture of affairs, they were ftill impending, and might have been felt with greater force, and more fatal confequences, in proportion as the crifis of its arrival was more remote. Though the credit of paper-currency may be founded on opinion, the degree of credit poffeffed by every nation is in proportion to its wealth. Its wealth confifts in the number of its hands, the quantity of its induftry, the value of its products, the conveniency, extent, and fecurity of its commerce. By thefe circumftances, and not by the temporary fluctuations of paper-currency, the world will eftimate the ftability and extent of public credit. It muft, however, be confeffed, that banking has an indirect tendency to throw the balance of trade againft a nation, and thus to hurt or deftroy its credit. But, for refearches of this kind, you may confult Mr David Hume's Effays, and the admirable treatife on Political Oeconomy by Sir James Stewart. The queftion is not, Whether banking be fatal or falutary to a nation ; but whether fuch a nation acts according to found policy, in its endeavours to retain its difputed rights, and to retard a feparation which muft fooner or later have happened, whether fhe had attempted to affert her claims or not ? If we cannot prevent the day of evil, it is certainly our next political refource to fufpend it.

SECT. IV. Our enfuing tafk is, to examine how far the honour of the nation is affected by the war with America. And here the Doctor

Doctor exerts great fagacity, in making the diftinction between the nation and its rulers. They certainly are perfonally diftinct, but politically one. In no free government under heaven, have the opinion of the nation and its rulers been exactly and perpetually unanimous. Nor is it poffible that they ever can be fo. Yet, in all political tranfactions with free ftates, the fenfe of government has always been, and muft always be, efteemed the fenfe of the nation. For if, upon any particular emergency, individuals are intitled to reject the fenfe of their reprefentatives, Why is not one as much intitled as another? Who fhall reconcile the infinite diverfities of opinion which muft then take place? and, till they are reconciled, upon what principles can political negociatiqns proceed; or by what public faith can they be ratified? The Doctor's politics may perhaps be the politics of Locke; but fenfe and reafon, practice and experience, God and nature, explode them. The fenfe of its legiflature is, therefore, to every political purpofe, the fenfe of the nation; and all the difhonour which can fall upon the one, for humiliating conceffions, and retracted meafures, will be juftly inflicted on the other.

Long has the imbecillity, the defultory conduct of Great Britain, been fufficiently ridiculous and contemptible to Europe. Let us not fink beneath the degree of contempt and ridicule which at prefent we fuffer. Let us not, in political quantity, become equal to Zero.

But, we are told, that it is no lefs prudent than honourable to retract. For, one day, our diftrefs may extort what our humanity and juftice deny. When the fky falls, fays the old adage, you may catch larks; but, he who waits till that event for his dinner, will difcover no high degree of prudence. The fubjection of Corfica to the Genoefe, was indeed the fubjection of one people to another. It was never undifturbed, never perpetual and confirmed. When the Genoefe found it impoffible to retain their dominions, they fold it to France. Is this agreeable to the prefent fpirit and conduct of Britain? The man who could, draw the comparifon, muft have neither honour nor modefty.

Is there no diftinction, then, between foreigners and defcendents? Are both to be treated in the fame manner? Is it reafonable to expect from the former what we may juftly demand from the latter? It has already been proved, that the diverfities between Britain and America are not fufficient to render them diftinct countries. But, till their characters, manners, laws, and interefts, be afcertained as incompatible in the fame civil fociety, our author's argument proves nothing at all.

The Dutch did not attempt to fhake off the yoke of Spain, without the higheft provocation. Their properties were not plundered by law, but by open force. The reprefentatives of their moft ancient and noble families were dragged to execution without trials,

and

and their heads expofed in every market-place. Their towns wero rather like flaughter-houfes and fhambles, than reforts of commerce and fecurity. Were hoftilities of this kind practifed in America prior to her refiftence? Are they now practifed, though in a ftate of war? If Dr Price imagines the United Provinces a republic fo happy, why does he not leave the Britifh conftitution, in its degeneracy, to become a member of that auguft and patriotic fociety? If he fhould take a refolution, fo becoming his nature and his principles, let him liften to the advice of a friend : Let him beware of fpeaking or writing concerning Dutch politics with the fame freedom which he has ufed in canvaffing thofe of Britain, unlefs he fhould chufe to become an honourable exile, or a more honourable mar-tyr, in the caufe of liberty.—The wars of Athens, and of Rome, are nothing to the prefent queftion.

‘ The prefent conteft with America is neither difgraceful to us, ‘ becaufe inconfiftent with our own feelings in fimilar cafes ; nor ‘ becaufe condemned by our own practice in former times.’ The ftruggles of Britain for liberty, were either againft foreign ufurpa-tion, or domeftic tyranny. Thofe of America are againft the legal demands of that very ftate, with which fhe is incorporated, and of which fhe conftitutes a part. But our author’s clemency is inimi-table and incomprehenfible. Becaufe others have vices fimilar to our own virtues in extreme, thefe vices muft not only be forgiven, but applauded. Once it happened, that a famous oeconomift feized a thief in the very act of purloining his property. Nobly done, faid he ; it is my bufinefs to fave, and your’s to gain. Our fpirits are congenial and fympathetic. I therefore not only pardon, but commend your actions, From henceforth, you fhall find my houfe, at all times, acceffible, and my good offices always at your com-mand. In return for thefe favours, I only afk your intercourfe and your gratitude. The felon demonftrated the fincerity with which he accepted thefe overtures, by the ufe which he made of them.

But the war, it feems, is difgraceful, on account of the manner in which it is carried on. The laws and religion of France have been eftablifhed in Canada. The negroes have been tempted to in-furrection. The Indians have been follicited to join us. We have tried to procure a body of Ruffians. Our own troops have been employed againft America ; and the defence of our forts and gar-rifons have been trufted in the hands of Germans. Upon the firft of thefe topics, I have already delivered my fentiments, much to the honour of Englifh toleration. Till the Doctor has given us better authority for the feduction of the flaves, than mere American reports, he muft permit us to doubt both their teftimony and his own. Indeed, the pamphlet before us is not calculated to infpire favourable prepoffeffions of his veracity. Were it true, that the In-dians had been folicited to join us, where is the article, either in the laws of war or of honour, which has been infringed by fuch a

pro-

procedure? Or, if the laws of war had been violated by it, whence is rebellion intitled to claim the immunities derived from them? If, in extraordinary emergencies, ministers must have recourse to extraordinary expedients, let the disgrace and odium fall upon such as deserve it. Why is the nation disarmed of troops at home, by that execrable jealousy and suspicion which are the eternal and essential inmates of mean and contracted spirits? Does that nation deserve less than contempt and perdition, which dares not to trust itself with its own defence? In hands like these, power is more despicable than impotence, and caution more ridiculous than folly. Let it be recorded, in the archives of eternity, to the glory of English valour, that she has neither courage to trust herself, nor to employ others in her own protection.

Sect. V. How far the present rupture with America is consistent with our sense of honour and justice, with the principles of our constitution, or with sound policy, we have examined, or rather conducted the Doctor through his examination. It remains that we pursue him, whilst he investigates the probability of our success. We are told, upon the Doctor's information, that the greatest number of troops which can be sent to America, inclusive of foreigners, is 30,000; to which the Doctor, in the excess of his generosity, adds 10 more. We shall reckon him a patriot, indeed, if he will realize the supposition; if he will collect them, and arm them, at his own expence. But this is more than government can expect, even from a welwisher so constant and zealous as himself, though his laudable endeavours to reconcile domestic discontents, and suppress the murmurs of faction, might give reason to expect much. But, with the 30,000 employed by government, and the 10,000 levied by himself, we must, it seems, encounter 500,000, or, in his own majestic phrase, half a million of effective men, fighting on their own ground, and engaged *pro focis et aris*. It may, however, be shrewdly suspected, that the Americans would not be sorry to find the seat of war transferred to another region, even at the expence of every advantage which they can reap from fighting on their own ground. But, while this mighty number of effective men are employed in the field, may we not modestly ask, who shall cultivate the land, and prepare its product for sale? who shall perform the other indispensible offices of commerce? Who shall superintend the growing state, and watch, with paternal care, *ne quid respublica detrimenti capeat?* When these tasks are properly fulfilled, there is reason to apprehend, that mighty deductions must be made from our 500,000. We may likewise ask the Doctor, in a friendly manner, whether his allies are sufficiently provided with the materials of subsistence, or with warlike stores? But, in these they will doubtless be abundantly supplied, by their captures

from

from Great Britain, or by their happy intelligence and intercourse with her enemies.

We might farther inquire, what money America possesses in her banks? what quantity she circulates? and how the credit of her paper-currency is likely to be maintained, during the cessation of trade? These questions might perhaps puzzle an Oedipus, but may receive an easy solution from the Doctor, and his patriotic sages.

Unhappy Britain, if the representation of thy patriots be true, immersed in luxury, poverty, and slavery, at home, and engaged in war abroad, with a power, not only sufficient to conquer, but annihilate thy forces, how shalt thou maintain thy ground, when Athens and Syracuse, Rome and the Italian states, Spain and the Netherlands, heaven and earth, the living and the dead, are invoked as the auxiliaries of thy enemies? Yet, let not these adverse circumstances drive thee to despair. The Americans are not invincible, even on their own ground. The wretched creatures who groan beneath their tyranny, are more than sufficient for the conquest, and will doubtless, in time, without sollicitation, collect and exert their force, to retaliate the injuries they have suffered. Troops and provisions have crossed the Atlantic in safety. How else did the progenitors of those, whose future atchievements are so loudly thundered in our ears, reach the continent? But whence has our author learned, that the troops employed in America are incapable of being recruited after any discomfiture? Have not the British armies, on former occasions, been defeated and reinforced? and why not now, as in other periods? Why not in America as in other places? Is either our native strength, or the friendship of our allies exhausted? Whatever denomination language may apply to our conduct, it certainly wants powers to describe the impudence of those who accuse us.

It is a precious political discovery, that a naval force, which cannot fail by land, is useless. Surely the Royal Society, who formerly elected our author a member, cannot now do less than create him their president. The maritime towns on the continent which are burnt or destroyed, may not, however, prove so many pledges of its fidelity lost. For, if rebuilt at all, their situation will probably be chosen by Great Britain.

Another of the inscrutable arcana for which we are indebted to the Doctor's wisdom, is, the facility of turning mercantile vessels into ships of war; and, by this manoeuvre, producing a formidable maritime power. But, when thus victorious, thus respectable by sea and land, what will British acts of parliament avail for intercepting the trade, and preserving the virtue and simplicity of America? Will they not unfurl their sails to every wind of heaven, and import every luxury which their commodities can purchase? We may safely admit the testimony of our author's acquaintance, that

he

he is free, or his own, that he is not free from fuperftition. The
courfe of nature, and the war with America, will not probably be
much influenced by either of thefe alternatives. Let us, however,
attend to the important birth with which the fpirit of our author
feems in labour, and which makes fuch a mighty ftruggle for deli-
very.

The dreadful impiety with which we are now charged, the a-
larming defcription of our manners and purfuits, are equally real
and melancholy. Would to God, my country had left it in my
power to confront the obfervations upon this, as upon other topics.
But, fhould I attempt an enterprize fo wild and impracticable,
truth, eternal and inflexible truth, would be my adverfary. But
lewdnefs, avarice, diffipation, and perjury here, are not more pre-
valent than hypocrify, and falfe devotion, in America. Bofton has
long been the capital feat of its religious fervors. Yet, I can af-
fure you, upon the authority of names as refpectable as America
can boaft, that, for want of probity and integrity, the Boftonians
are infamous, even to a proverb. Nay, that any perfon, whether
from the iflands or the continent, will be more readily and implicitly trufted in bufinefs than they. Thus is the Creator and Judge
of the univerfe flattered and cajolled, in hopes that he may forgive
the impofitions practifed, and the injuries inflicted on his creatures.
Such are the faftings and prayers offered to the throne of Omnifci-
ence by North America. ' Which fide then is Providence likely
' to favour ?'

If the caufe of public juftice be the caufe of God, Why may we
not implore his blessing upon ours ? If we only act for the main-
tenance of our native rights, Why may we not affirm, in his pre-
fence, that we are not the aggreffors ? Government will readily
acknowledge, that its prefent efforts are not in defence of perfonal
rights and properties : That it fights not to repel the immediate
hand of oppreffive power, but to preferve its integrity, and vindicate
its legal rights. Thefe are circumftances, in which private liti-
gants may make large conceffions ; and, in doing fo, will act agreeably to the fpirit of their religion. But, fhould the fame rule be
extended to the adminiftration of kingdoms, deftruction muft be its
obvious and neceffary confequence. For, in proportion as the government recedes, the fubject will incroach ; the hands of the executive power will be weakened ; the ftrength of its oppofers increa-
fed and reinforced ; extraneous foes will impute its lenient meafures
to timidity or weaknefs ; infult, rapine, and cruelty, will univerfally prevail. Befides, every government is accountable to God
and pofterity for the truft repofed in it by its conftituents ; and e-
very right which it facrifices to mercenary ends, to factious views,
or to the fuggeftions of cowardice, will be amply vindicated by the
courfe of events in this world, and by the divine adminiftration in
the next. Let the Doctor, therefore, who fo warmly exorts his

readers, remember, that, though the profufe or wanton effufion of blood be a fin which cries to heaven for vengeance; yet the public incendiary, who deftroys that union and confidence which are effential to the order of ftates, and the fubfiftence of government, fhall not efcape with impunity.

——*Procul, O procul, efte profani !* Let us now liften with reverence and attention to our author's recapitulation of his arguments, and to the feelings of his heart. But, as you have his book before you, it will be fufficient for me to anfwer, without rehearfing the fummary account of his former reafoning, which concludes the fection. When, or where has it been pretended, that the Americans are more our fubjects than we theirs ? The colonies are indeed fubject to our legiflature, but fo likewife are we ourfelves. If fuch people as are only virtually reprefented cannot be taxed by themfelves, then are two thirds of the inhabitants of Great Britain taxed by a power extrinfic to themfelves, and confequently flaves. If the nature of government requires, that people fhould be taxed by virtual reprefentation, every one who fubmits to live under fuch an oeconomy, is really taxed by himfelf; and, as the Americans are virtually reprefented in the Britifh legiflature, they are virtually taxed by themfelves. Miftakes and inconveniencies will happen in all human governments ; it cannot, therefore, be imagined, that taxes will always be levied with prudence and moderation ; nor, even that the exigences of the ftate will be always proportioned to the abilities of the people. But, the reciprocation of interefts between Britain and her colonies muft effectually reftrain all exorbitant demands upon them, if fhe would preferve the original fources of her opulence, in a proper condition, to yield her copious and permanent fupplies.

Whofe parliament, and whofe laws have the Americans then refufed to obey ? A parliament and laws which are as much their own as ours. ' The lands of our freeholders are reprefented, not ' theirs,' fays the Doctor. Is it then the particles of earth, or the ftones of houfes that are reprefented ; or the people who inhabit them ? Are the cares of a reprefentative confined to the diftrict which he reprefents ? Is it not his bufinefs to adjuft the intereft of fubordinate communities with the general intereft of the whole fociety ? Is he then exclufively elected for his particular province, and for thofe alone by whofe voices he was chofen ; or as a delegate for the whole province, and a fuperintendant of the general welfare ? Why then fhould not the fame delegated powers virtually extend to the continent, which is a part of the Britifh empire, as well as to thofe in Britain, who have no vote ? If political liberty be only commenfurate with actual reprefentation, then is liberty a mere *ens rationis ;* as elections for reprefentatives by poll, if practicable, would not be eligible ; or, if eligible, would not be practicable. .

Had the authority of American affemblies and councils been felf-derived and independent ; had America and this ifland been different ftates, all our prefent claims muft have been ufurpations, and all the expoftulations of our author juft and reafonable. But, founded as they are upon falfe fuppofitions, they ftand refuted by themfelves, and prove nothing but the malignity or folly of the inventors. It is too true, that we may perceive ' a growing inter-' courfe between the court and parliament.' But when has it awed minifters of ftate with propriety ? At that period, when its power and infolence were in their zenith. What was the refult ? We exchanged an ambitious monarch for a tyrannical protector; and the Ottoman court was lefs defpotic than the Britifh republic. I do not mention this as a detraction from the merit and importance of parliaments. On the contrary, I think liberty effential to government, and parliaments effential to liberty ; but, like every other human inftitution, they are imperfect, and fufceptible of degeneracy. In the times of Henry VIII. and his daughter Elifabeth, when the found of liberty was as high in England as at prefent, What could be more obfequious to royal pleafure, than the parliament ? Every compliance, which is now obtained by corruption, was then extorted by terror. But, whatever be the prefent intercourfe between the court and parliament, if each of them has acted within the limits of its proper department ; if the King has not limited parliamentary prerogatives, nor the. parliament betrayed the interefts of its conftituents, it ill becomes a fubject, either to refift or complain. The colonifts have no longer left their aims to fuppofition and conjecture. One of the delegates, in their grand provincial congrefs, has publifhed their intention, and given reafons for it. If we confider the terms ftipulated by their public declarations, to what lefs than abfolute independence can they amount ? Though it fhould be proved, that we, or fome other ftate equally powerful, muft be effential to the fubfiftence of the colonies, Who informed the Doctor that they would return to us ? And, though it fhould be poffible, as I hope it is, for us to fubfift without them, can it be concluded from thence, that our government fhould relinquifh its juft rights, or humbly follicit compliances, which it is intitled to demand ?—A gentleman of a thoufand *per annum ;* may perhaps fubfift upon five hundred, is he, for that reafon, morally obliged to refign half his fortune, or to cringe and flatter thofe who would take it from him, for the privilege of retaining it ?

It has been repeatedly acknowledged, that, whenever the period fhall arrive, in which the colonies are found capable of fupplying their wants, of protecting their ftate, and of regulating their affairs, this muft be the crifis of their political maturity ; this the time of their emancipation from parental controul. But it will not be pretended that this is their fituation at prefent. Where is the government which can be rendered accountable for the cruelty and avarice of

individuals,

individuals, when too distant to be reached by its influence ? The miserable inhabitants of the East-Indies have too much reason to hold particular Englishmen in execration. But such a curse can never be justly transferred to any government, for crimes which it neither authorifed nor understood.

In the 37th page of the pamphlet before us, the Doctor seems impreffed with strong anticipations of some great end, some distinguished epoch in providence, to refult from the prefent agitations in Britain and America. This millenary fcheme, which, in that paffage, he obfcurely hints, is now more extenfively difplayed. Its forefts, its mountains, and its rivers, are now beheld in perfpective ; and nothing remains but the extermination of Great Britain, and a total revolution in the policy of Europe, to evolve the whole majeftic fcheme in all its luftre and beauty. I am fo much enamoured of this excellent plan, that it is my ardent wifh, and real intention, to importune fome famous fage, profoundly fkilled in Roficrucian lore, or fome other way converfant with fuperior intelligencies, that he may call to folemn council the genii of nations, and procure fome high office for one of my pofterity in this new republic. But perhaps I may be miftaken ; poffibly there may then be no neceffity for government. Every thing may be in a ftate of nature. The laws of order, benevolence, and rectitude, may univerfally prevail by their native energy ; and no ftatutes, no injunctions be known, but fuch as are pronounced from the Temple of Wifdom, by the mouth of Liberty. Animated with this glorious profpect, let us pafs to the Doctor's conclufion.

CONCLUSION. The ends of our author's benevolence are not fufficiently anfwered, by expofing the injuftice, abfurdity, difhonour, and danger of our war with America, unlefs he propofes fome plan of reconciliation. But, diffident of his own talents, he chufes to tranfcribe thofe terms of accommodation from the fpeech of a diftinguifhed peer. Thefe terms might indeed conftitute the articles of alliance between different and independent ftates ; but can never be ftipulated by capitulation from any community of the fame ftate, nor granted by treaty to that community. What prerogative or advantage could America lofe by the eftablifhment of thefe articles, for which fhe might not contend as an independent ftate ? What could Britain gain, to which it is not already intitled by an inherent right ? In a word, fuppofing the terms fuggefted by his Lordfhip were ratified, both in Britain and America, In what circumftances would they differ from independent kingdoms, allied by treaty, and regulating their political or commercial intercourfe in fuch a manner, as that each might derive the greateft advantage from both ? But, however liberal the conceffions made by Great Britain to America, in this conciliatory plan, nothing is more certain, than that all overtures of this kind would have been refufed. America is wife

wife enough to fee, that the independence of a ftate muft be intrinfic, and can never derive permanence or fecurity from political negociations alone, by whatever fanctions they may be guaranteed.
Every independence, therefore, which the colonies cannot acquire
and mantain by their own internal force, is evanefcent and fluctuating, as the breath which compofed the words that expreffed
them. If, therefore, independence was their object, it could only
be acquired and maintained by fuccefsful refiftence.

I deplore, with Dr Price, the growing evils of national-debt and
corruption. I deplore the rapid progrefs, and univerfal dominion
of vice and impiety. But I cannot perceive that, even on account
of thefe calamities, it became neceffary for government to decline
the war with America, by a diflionourable retreat; A retreat
which muft have given the fignal of attack to all the other powers
of Europe, to whofe confpiring efforts we might have fallen an un-
refifting prey.

Our author, in his appendix, ftates the national expenditure and
income for eleven years, from 1764 to 1774; But, as I have reafon to believe the facts upon which thefe calculations proceed in-
accurately reprefented, the calculations themfelves are ineffectual,
and can by no means merit our confidence. Thofe who are engaged in trade, or in the finances, may, if they have leifure and
inclination, inveftigate the reality of the Doctor's premiffes, and
the accuracy of his deductions. But, as they feem to me remotely,
if at all connected with the prefent controverfy, I am neither engaged by duty nor inclination to explore them.

Thus have I given you my firft thoughts upon the fubject, in the
firft expreffions which occurred. It will furprife you to find them
fo much protracted, both beyond your expectation and my own.
Notwithftanding this, I cannot omit the prefent opportunity of ob-
ferving, that few conjunctures could have been more favourable to
a country long accumulated with infults, or abandoned to negli-
gence and fcorn, than that which is now prefented. In former
times, when the native ferocity of England was ftill more inflated
by domeftic fecurity and foreign conqueft, we had no reafon to be
furprifed, that the efforts of Scotland to be reinftated in a capacity
for felf-defence were ineffectual, though fhe had regularly difchar-
ged the taxes impofed, and contributed to the revenue her full proportion, as ftipulated by the articles of union.

But, in the prefent fituation of affairs, when England is embroiled with her colonies, and far from being fecure that the other ftates
of Europe will obferve a facred neutrality, that overtures for increafing the means of internal fecurity have been neglected and
defpifed, every man of fenfe and honour muft perceive with equal
aftonifhment and indignation.

Had our anceftors been able to transfer their gallant fouls, by the
fame inheritance with their names and eftates, could we have fuffered

fered such a repulse with patience ? But our spirits are become tame
and tractible ; we are sufficiently domesticated, and moulded to the
inclinations of our masters. If they vouchsafe to allow us the per-
quisites of a luxurious table, we can not only endure to be kicked
and buffeted, but are even sufficiently obsequious to kiss the foot
that spurns us. : Heaven and earth ! Are we men ? Are we Scots-
men ? Are we the descendants of those heroes whom neither Rome
nor England could subdue ; and can the lust of wealth and pleasure
subjugate our spirits to this degree of meanness ?—We have been
no less publicly than falsely branded with a predilection for despotism ;
Would to the Almighty this were the only chain that held us ! Soon
would that insolence, which could thus upbraid us in a public and
judicial capacity, retract an assertion so dishonourable, and, by the
baseness of its fear, discover the enormity of its guilt.

I am by no means for dissolving solemn treaties with temerity.
Let us still continue the inseparable friends and allies of England ;
but let us at the same time take care to preserve the importance and
dignity of friends and allies. If we act with that degree of spirit
and magnanimity which becomes our ancestors and ourselves, the
haughty and imperious power which now insults us will tremble to
its basis at the prospect of an impending rupture. But the subject
is too interesting, *and I grow warm*. Forgive this excursion, and
believe me, with all the tenderness which that endearing name can
imply, .

Your most faithful

And affectionate friend,

Valerius Corvinus.

Postscript. Since the above remarks were written, I have
seen An Inquiry whether the Guilt of the present Civil War in
America ought to be imputed to Great Britain or America, by John
Roebuck, M. D. F. R. S. It is a masterly, elegant, and irresistible
performance ; and, as most of the positions which I have endeavoured to establish, are there illustrated and confirmed by unque-
stionable facts, I must recommend this short, but valuable tract, to
your most serious and attentive consideration.

www.ingramcontent.com/pod-product-compliance
Lightning Source LLC
Chambersburg PA
CBHW032344020726
47499CB00009B/3168